BEST OF YOU

BEST OF YOU

A Colorado Black Diamonds Novel

EMILY SILVER

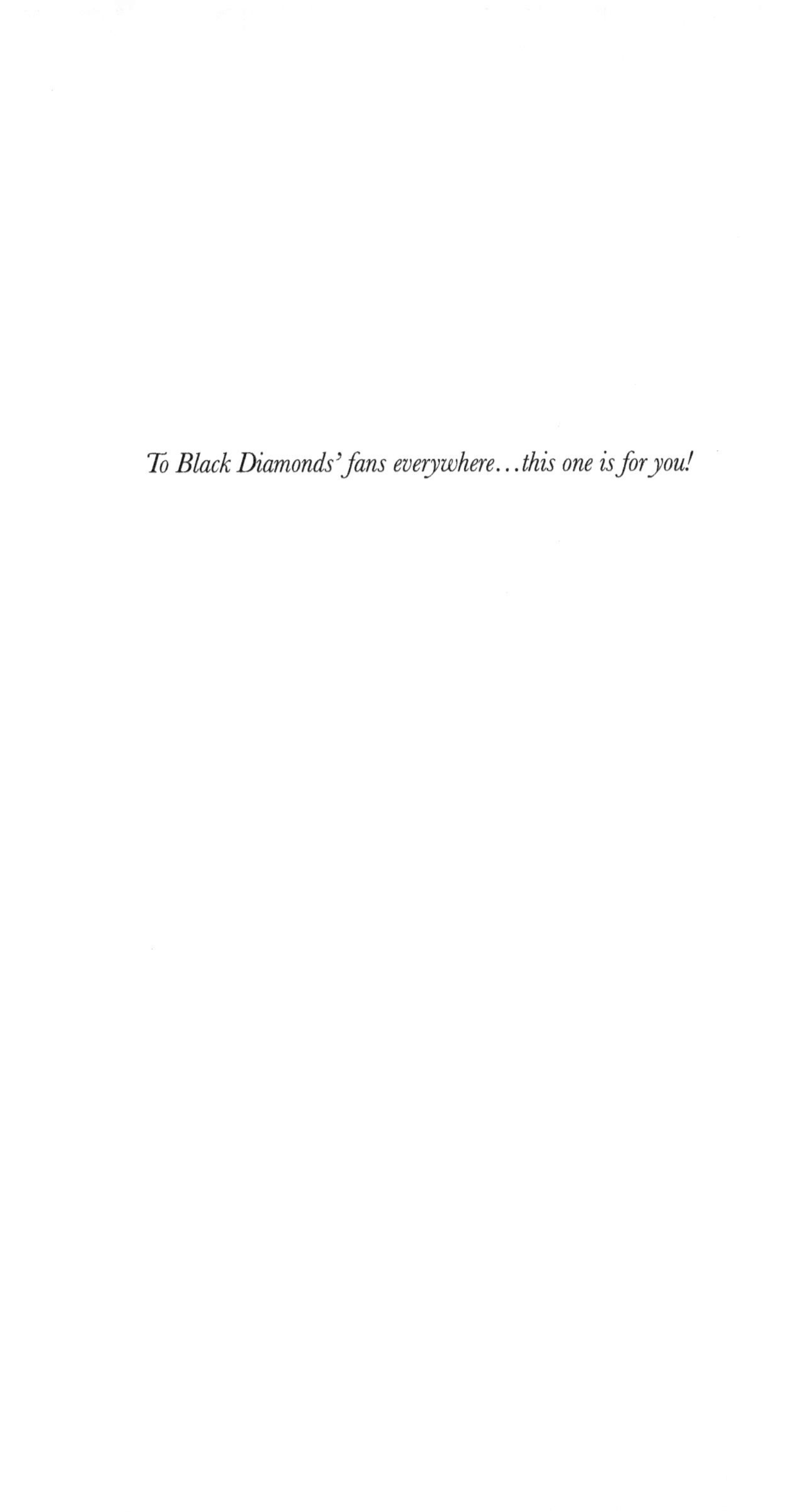

To Black Diamonds' fans everywhere…this one is for you!

DECLAN

"More shots!"

"Bro, the bottle is empty. I don't need anymore." I clap my friend on the shoulder and drain what's left in my red cup. "I'll stick with beer."

"You're so lame."

"I have an early flight home. No way I'm dragging my hungover ass onto a plane."

Flipping him off, I make my way through the maze of people in the living room toward the kitchen. The line for the keg is long, but I skip to the front.

Perks of the party being at our house.

With it being the last night of school, we decided to go all out. Since our team is the most popular on campus, it brings everyone out in droves.

"Hey, Declan. Want to go upstairs?" a girl asks from where she's sitting on the kitchen counter.

"Sorry. Just need a refresher." Grabbing the hose, I top off my drink and head back into the house.

Music shakes the walls. Christmas lights hang from the

ceiling. The stench of sweat and alcohol linger. Our house is the place to be tonight.

Squeezing through the masses, I bound up the stairs, needing to hit the bathroom. Turning the corner, a small woman bumps into me. What remains in her cup spills down the front of my shirt.

"Oh God. I'm so sorry." Her gaze flits up to meet mine and her jaw drops. "Wow. You're pretty."

"I could say the same about you."

Long, blonde hair curls down over her shoulders. Blue eyes are hidden behind thin, round glasses. There is nothing sexy about the overalls she's wearing, but damn, she somehow makes them look good.

"You should probably change your shirt." Her warm hand tries to wipe up the alcohol now dampening the front.

"It's fine." I grab her hand to stop her, holding it against my abs.

Is it shameless? Yes. But I don't care.

Because this woman is stunning. Even my liquored-up brain realizes this.

"Wow. You're really pretty. Like really, *really*, pretty."

I smirk down at her. "So you've said."

"You're a ranunculus."

"What?" This woman is fucking gorgeous, but I have no idea what she's saying. Likely a result of all the drinks I've had tonight.

"A frog."

"I'm sorry, what?" I couldn't have heard her correctly. "A frog?"

"You're not listening to me." Her words slur together. I don't know if it's her, or the haze of my own buzz. "You're attractive. Like the ranunculus."

"What's this...rancoolous?"

She rolls those pretty blue eyes at me. "It's a flower."

"So I'm a frog flower?" I ask her.

"Ugh. Pretty guys never get it."

"I don't think you're explaining it right," I argue. "Besides, if we're going to continue discussing this, I need to know your name."

"Alice."

"Alice. I'm Declan."

"Okay, Declan. Why aren't you understanding my little frog flower?"

"Is it a frog sitting on a flower?"

Alice sways and I shift us so she's leaning against the wall. "Ugh. I'm too drunk to be having this conversation."

"I think we both are."

"I never drink this much." Alice points a finger in my face.

"Why are you drinking this much tonight then?"

Standing like this, I'm a full head taller than she is. "Stupid family stuff."

"Care to expand on stupid family stuff, Alice?"

She shakes her head then winces. "No. You're still a stranger."

"You've now called me a frog and spilled your drink all over me. I'd say we're friends now."

"Maybe if I kiss you, you'll turn into a prince." Her blue eyes grow wide under her glasses. "Oh God. I didn't mean to say that."

I smirk. "Are you saying I'm not a prince?"

"I mean, you're really pretty. All princes are pretty."

"You're still going with pretty?"

"Declan, you are too good-looking for your own good. That's why you're a ranunculus."

"You keep saying this."

"*You* keep saying this," she parrots back at me.

"You're a little tipsy," I tell her. "Do you want some water?"

"I—"

Her face turns green as her hand flies up to cover her mouth.

"Oh shit. Are you—"

She pukes. All down the front of me.

"Oh God." I gag. I bury my face in the crook of my elbow to try and stop myself from doing the exact same thing.

"Oh my God." On top of still looking green, she looks more embarrassed now. "I can't believe I did that. I'm going to go die in shame."

Grabbing the cup in her hand, I set it on the floor next to me and take her hand in mine. "C'mon. Let's go get you some water and you can sleep it off in my room."

"I am not sleeping with you." Alice digs her heels in so she isn't moving.

"Did I say that?" I turn back to face her.

"Gross. Did I just step in vomit?" someone shrieks behind us.

"You're coming with me." I scoop Alice up into my arms and take her to the bedroom at the end of the hallway.

Shutting the door behind me, the noise of the party is muted. I set Alice on her feet and walk over to my dresser. Stripping out of my T-shirt and jeans, I grab a pair of clean sweats and shirt to change into. Heading into the bathroom, I grab my mouth wash to give her.

One perk of the house – I only have to share a bathroom with one other guy.

"We're not sleeping together," Alice tells me again, taking the rinse into the bathroom with her.

"Trust me. I don't sleep with drunk girls." I pull the soft

cotton shirt over my head. "I don't want to smell like puke."

"Ugh." She buries her face in her hands as she walks out. "I'm so sorry."

"Do you want a shirt to sleep in?"

One blue eye peeks out between her fingers. "No. I should really get home." She sighs. "I don't like spending the night in strangers' beds."

"I can't drive and there's no way I'm letting you get home on your own."

"I can grab a ride share."

I shake my head and pull her hands away from her face. "No. I don't want anyone taking advantage of you."

"But—"

I hold up two fingers. "Scout's honor. You can sleep it off here, and I'll make sure you get home in the morning."

She eyes me before giving me a slight nod. I'm guessing anything more and she'd be worshipping the porcelain god again.

"Fine." Alice sits on my haphazardly made bed. "But where are you going to sleep?"

I grab one of the pillows on my bed and the blanket on the end. "On the floor."

"Like a prince."

"I'll make sure you get home once you're feeling better." I brush the hair off her forehead and pull her glasses off her face as she lies down on the bed. Her eyelashes kiss the tops of her cheeks.

Fuck. She is so damn beautiful, it hurts.

"Thanks, Declan. I'm sorry I puked on you."

"I'm not."

"Really?"

"Nope." I shake my head. The buzz is already starting to wear off. Perks of being a college kid with a high tolerance. "I can honestly say this was the best night of the year."

"Now I know you're lying."

"Who me? I never lie."

Alice laughs and it hits me square in the gut. It's the sweetest sound I think I've ever heard. Better than the sound of skates on ice.

She yawns. "Such a charmer."

"Go to sleep, Froggie. I'll make sure you're okay." I flick off the light and stretch out on the floor. "Just make sure if you need to puke again, you lean the other way."

"Such a charmer."

Chapter One

"Fucking champs, baby!"

Knocking shot glasses with Cash, I glug back the tequila shot. I've lost track of how many I've had tonight. When you win the Stanley Cup, you're allowed to have as many as you want.

"Couldn't have done it without you, Paddy!" Cash kisses my temple after he finishes his own. "That last goal in the third was a thing of beauty."

I smile, thinking about the errant shot that somehow ended up in the back of the net, sealing our victory. On home ice, no less.

The gleaming cup is sitting on top of the bar. Everyone has been crowded around it all night. After each of us drank champagne from it in the locker room, we moved the after-party to a nearby bar that Bex reserved for us.

"Hey, you set me up for it."

"Nah. All you, kid."

"Kid? You realize I'm the same age as you, right?"

Cash waves me off. "You just got here. You feel like a kid to me."

"Well, this kid needs more shots." I flag down the bartender and order two more.

"Don't you two think you've had enough?" Piper, Cash's girlfriend sidles up to him and wraps her arms around his waist.

"How many times do we get to celebrate a Stanley Cup, Princess?" Cash asks her.

"Well, considering this is the second time in two years, I'd say the chances are good."

The bartender drops off the two shots and I hold them up. "All the more reason to take them." ·

"One more and then we can go home," Cash tells her, pressing a kiss to the crown of her head. "We have to celebrate on our own."

"And I'm out." I take the shot and slam the glass on the wooden bar top.

The two of them don't even notice I'm gone, swept up in their own love bubble. Staggering away from the bar, I know I'm at my limit.

But fuck, who cares? I've never won anything before.

Peewee hockey? Always came in second.

Frozen Four? Never even came close in college.

Nashville Knights? I don't think our coach knew what the term winning meant.

This is the best feeling in the world.

Spotting a blonde head over the rest of the crowd, I head in that direction. I'd recognize that bun anywhere. Even drunk.

"Hey, Froggie."

"Hey, champ."

Scooching into the booth that Alice is sitting in, I rest my head on the table. "New nickname?"

She shrugs a shoulder. "For now. Until you lose the title."

"Ouch." I laugh. "Guess I have to work hard to keep my nickname."

Alice brushes a lock of hair off my forehead. I peek one eye up at her. She looks tired. At this late hour, how could she not be?

We've been at the bar for hours. Looking at my watch, it's pushing three in the morning. "Don't you have to work tomorrow?"

Alice shakes her head, sipping on her water. "Nope. I told Leon I was going to be celebrating with you."

"Awfully certain that we were going to win."

"I mean, have you seen the talent on this team? You would've been hard to beat."

The bar is still crowded. No one wants to leave. I know as well as the next person that this same group of guys won't be here next year. Hell, I've only been here a few months. Nothing is a given in this league.

"I still can't believe we won it, Alice."

"I'm really proud of you, Dec," she tells me. "Thanks for letting me be here."

I reach over the table and grab her hand, squeezing it. "If you hadn't come, I would have dragged you here myself."

"Good."

"Besides, my parents couldn't hang. They left for the hotel hours ago."

Alice laughs. "The only reason I'm still here is because I didn't want to leave you on your own."

"I'm not on my own. The team is still here."

"You know what I mean."

"You can leave if you want."

"I'm okay," she tells me.

She's fading and fading fast. "Why don't we both head home?"

"No. I want you to stay."

"Nope." I motion to her water glass and she passes it over for me to drink the last of it down. "Let's go."

"Want me to call a car?" Alice asks, slinging her bag over her shoulder. My championship hat still rests on her head. She looks fucking adorable.

"Yes please."

Thank God that Bex arranged rides for everyone tonight. The last thing I want to do is try to figure out getting home tonight.

I hug every single guy as the two of us leave the crowded bar.

I slump over her as we wait outside the bar. Even though it's late, people are still out celebrating. Two cups in as many years? Yeah, people are fucking ecstatic.

"There he is," Alice points out. A black SUV pulls up to the curb.

Swinging open the back door, I slide in as Alice gets in next to me. My head falls into her lap as exhaustion takes over.

"Thanks for taking us home," I hear Alice tell the driver.

They carry on a quiet conversation as I let the happy buzz of alcohol fill my veins. I don't remember a time when I've ever felt this good. Sure, maybe when I got drafted, but this? I want to hang onto this feeling for as long as possible.

"Spend the night with me?" I ask my best friend as the car rolls its way closer to my house. I can't wait to get into bed and crash.

She smiles down at me. "I don't sleep with strangers."

"Good thing I'm not a stranger."

"You will be. You're going to become this big hotshot

NHL player now that you've won the cup and forget about little ol' me."

I crack one eye open at her. A smile lights up Alice's face. "Please. Like I could ever forget about you, Froggie."

She brushes a stray lock of hair off my forehead. "We're home."

"Thanks man," I say. With very little grace, I unbuckle myself and stumble out of the car.

"Congratulations, Mr. Paddack," the driver tells me.

Shutting the door, Alice wraps a supporting arm around my waist and hauls me inside.

Unlocking the door, Alice pushes it open with her hip and leads me straight to my room. I collapse onto the bed, wanting the mattress to swallow me whole. I kick off my shoes and nestle into the pillows.

"Do you need anything?" Alice asks as she pulls back the comforter and lies down next to me. Flipping onto my side, I turn to stare at her.

"Thanks for being my best friend, Froggie."

She smiles back at me. A smile I've grown to love every time I see it.

"Always."

Chapter Two

DECLAN

"How are you feeling today?" Cash asks as I drop down into my seat next to him.

I stretch my legs out in front of me. "Fuck, I could sleep for a week. I'm exhausted."

He shakes his head. "Whoever decided to have locker clean out a few days after the big win is a sadist."

"And the day after the championship parade? I need an IV to recover at this point."

It's been nonstop since we won. Celebrating every minute of each day since. Getting to carry the Cup through the streets of Denver and seeing the fans' excitement might have been the best moment since winning.

"Worse things in life," Cash points out.

"And we still get to look forward to our rings coming."

His smile grows. "Damn. Those are always fun to get."

"Novelty hasn't worn off yet?" I ask, grabbing my bag and starting to chuck everything from my locker into it.

Even though I've only been here since the trade deadline, my stall is a mess. I've managed to collect a mishmash of things since I got here.

I smile at the little frog that Alice gave me as a good luck charm before my first game I played here. I didn't see much ice time then, but it picked up the closer we got to the playoffs.

Trash cans are spread out through the locker room. Music is blasting through the open space. The cup is sitting in a place of honor in the front of the room.

I can't wait until I get my day with it.

Damn. It feels incredible to have won. I never thought I'd get to this point in my career, given I was playing for the Knights. We didn't have the best coach. He didn't seem to have much fire in him to win.

Playing for Colorado is a dream come true.

"Gentlemen." Coach Barney calls everyone's attention to him in the center of the locker room and the music shuts off. "I know there are going to be a lot more celebrations going on, but I wanted to take a minute and tell you how proud I am of you. You played a hell of a series. No game is a given. You earned every goal out there on the ice. This team was resilient through the ups and downs, and we came out on top."

Everyone starts clapping and cheering.

"I won't keep you, but I just wanted to say thank you. You made me look good out there. Take care of yourselves this offseason and I'll see you in a few months."

Coach Barney starts going around to talk to each of the guys, and I go back to finishing sorting out what's in my locker.

"So I've been thinking," Cash starts, dropping an empty stick of deodorant in the trash bin behind him.

"Don't hurt yourself." Troy laughs from his other side.

Cash flips him off and looks to me. "I'm thinking we need to celebrate our win."

That has me confused. "What have we been doing since? I thought those were damn good celebrations."

This also earns me a finger and Troy and I both laugh at him before Coach comes over to us, interrupting our conversation.

"Gentlemen. I'm assuming you know how to handle yourselves this offseason?"

"Yes, Coach," we all answer at the same time.

"Good." He claps me on the shoulder. "We were lucky to get you, Paddy. Couldn't have managed this run without you."

I'm beaming. I don't care if the smile on my face takes up my whole head. "Thanks. I still can't believe we won the Cup."

"Enjoy it. These don't come around often."

I nod at him as he continues moving down the line of guys.

"See?" Cash pulls my attention back to him. "Coach says we should enjoy the win, which leads me to what I was saying earlier. We should head to Vegas to have one big celebration."

Troy ponders the thought. "You know, I don't hate that idea."

"Wow, a ringing endorsement," Cash deadpans. "Who said I invited you?"

Troy scoffs, "I'm inviting myself then."

I laugh at the two of them. This is one of the reasons I loved getting traded here. The camaraderie is like nothing I've ever had. I had a close group of guys that I still miss in Nashville, but every member of the team has welcomed me here with open arms.

"I'm down to go."

Cash smiles at me. "See? Paddy here is invited."

"Fuck you." Troy laughs at him. "My wife is besties with your girlfriend. Of course we're coming."

"Hey. Can I come?" Nick walks over to us, hands on his hips.

"I mean, the goalie gets an automatic invite," Cash says. "All those saves you made to get us the Cup? Hell, I'll pay for your ticket."

A blush creeps up his neck. Something I've learned about Nick is he hates being in the spotlight. Even more so now because of his relationship with our GM.

"No need. Are the partners invited?" he asks.

"Yes. As if we could leave them at home," Cash tells him before turning to me. "Want to bring Alice?"

"I'd love to. I'll talk to her and see if her work schedule is clear."

"Awesome. Let's do it. Say, next weekend?" Cash asks, looking around.

"Works for me."

Once I finish clearing out my locker, I have the rest of the afternoon free, and I know Alice is at the shop. I'll drop in and see if she wants to come. Her schedule isn't as flexible, but I know her boss. Leon loves me. It'd only be two days off, and I want one last celebration with my best friend before it's time to come back down from the stratosphere.

Besides, how can she say no to her best friend?

Chapter Three

"Alice, where are we on the Banning wedding?" Leon asks.

Grabbing the clipboard hanging on the wall, I give it a quick scan. "Only the bridesmaids bouquets are left to do."

"Perfect. Let's get those wrapped up today so we can get them ready for delivery."

"Will do."

"And let me know what you want for lunch. Jacob is going to bring it by since we have our floral workshop tonight."

"Where is he going?"

"The new ramen place on Fifth."

My mouth waters at the thought of it. "I have been wanting to try it forever, but I haven't been able to get in."

Leon gives me a dazzling, white smile. His bald head shines bright under the overhead lights. Tattoos stretch down both arms under his red *Enchanted Petals* T-shirt. "You mean you can't get your bestie to get you an in?"

I wave him off. "You know I would never bother him during the playoffs."

"Honey, that man would do anything you asked him to."

I smile as I set the clipboard down and head to the cooler in the back of the store to grab flowers to start work. "Just because you got married doesn't mean everyone is loved up."

"I can't help it if I'm in the honeymoon phase and want everyone to be in love."

"Leon," I groan. "Please don't try setting me up again."

He waves me off. "I know, I know. You'd rather spend every night with your flowers than go out and enjoy life."

"Hey," I scoff. "I do not."

"Really?"

With one quirk of an eyebrow, I know I'm made.

"Sue me that I'm better with flowers than people."

"Because flowers don't talk back."

"More like flowers don't care that I'm awkward."

He laughs and strolls back to the office. Grabbing my apron off the hook, I grab a bundle of peonies and head to the workbench.

The perfume of flowers scents the air. Dried bouquets hang over the black-and-white diamond tiled floors. Refinished bookshelves line the walls that sell various candles and reed diffusers. Oversized buckets filled with fresh blooms take up the entirety of the main desk.

I get lost in my work, in finding the perfect colors to create a work of art. I create masterpieces for everyday life and moments to remember. This is why I love what I do. Why I have never wanted to do anything else in life.

The bell above the door chimes, pulling me away from the last bouquets I'm making. "Welcome to Enchanted Petals. How can I help you?"

"Hey, Froggie." I peer around the tall bundle and smile.

"What are you doing here?" I wipe my hands and step out from behind the bench to see Declan. He's twisting the Black Diamonds hat around on his head to face the back. In a pair of black joggers and a gray muscle tee, he's the epitome of casual.

"Can't I stop by and see you?"

"Declan, I saw you two days ago."

He shrugs. "I know, but I'm bored."

I smile. Of course he is. This is something I know about him. The first week or two of the offseason is always hard for him. Declan likes staying busy.

"Declan." Leon comes out front from the back. "Congrats on the cup thingy."

"Ugh." Another new voice enters the fray. "Did he really just call it a 'cup thingy'?"

Leon bats his eyelashes at his husband. A tall, older white man, his hair is a soft red with a few white strands peeking through.

"He really did." Declan winces. "I don't know how you married someone so anti-sports."

Jacob looks at Leon. "It's because he's cute.

"Damn right I am." Leon laughs. "Now, did you bring your cute husband and Alice lunch?"

Jacob sets a paper bag on the counter.

"Oh that smells delicious." Plastic containers are pulled out of the bag, filled to the brim. "Thanks for picking this up. I'm starving."

"If it weren't for me, I swear you two would forget to eat most days."

Opening the lid to the one with a big black A on the top, I breathe in the aroma of the broth and noodles.

Grabbing the spork from the bag, I stick it into the bowl and take a heaping, hot bite. "Oh my God."

"So ladylike," Declan tells me.

"Let me see you do it then." I hand over my utensil to him, savoring the sweet and salty taste of the noodles on my tongue.

"I actually did drop by for a reason." Declan takes the proffered sort of spoon from my hand and takes his own bite. Of course he slurps it up in one easy bite. The cocky smile he gives me tells me he knows it too.

"What's that?" I ask, taking the container back and going back to eating. There's no way I'm letting him have this.

"The guys invited me to go to Vegas with them."

"Really? That's great, Declan."

He smiles at me. The real one. Not the one that he shows off to the public. The one just for me. "I want you to come with me."

"What? I can't do that."

"Why not? Cash invited you. All of their wives and partners will be going."

I roll my eyes at him as I set my spork down. "Exactly. Partners. I'm your friend, Dec."

"Excuse me. Best friend." His tone is firm—not to be argued with. "And I want you there with me."

"I have work."

Declan smirks at me. "I didn't even tell you when it was."

"I have a wedding coming up in two weeks that I have to get ready for. Bouquets and centerpieces don't make themselves."

"Please?" Declan whines, clasping his hands under his chin. "I don't want to go alone."

I swat at his chest. "You won't be alone. You'll have the guys there."

"And that's not you, Froggie." He hops down off the counter and swivels his hat around toward the front. "I'll send you the dates. Think about it, okay? I want you there."

"Okay."

The chime over the door rings out and he's gone.

"Alice, honey. You have to go with him." Leon appears at my side as if out of nowhere.

"Where'd you come from?" I jump, knocking my elbow into a metal pail of flowers.

"Eavesdropping, obviously."

"Leon." I smack him in the chest and grab the stray flowers from the bucket and return to making my arrangements. "I cannot go to Vegas."

"Alice. Honey." Leon grabs my hand. "You never do anything for yourself."

"I do—"

"Do not argue with me. All you do is work. You need to live a little. When that sexy man asks you to go to Vegas, you don't think. You say yes."

"Leon. Declan is my best friend." Nothing like puking all over someone to bond you for life. Ever since freshman year in college, Declan has been one of the most important people in my life. I hated it when he was drafted by Nashville. I tried to see him as often as I could, but working at a flower shop didn't lend for a lot of days off. Especially during wedding season. Which turned into the holidays. Which turned right back into wedding season.

Never a dull moment in the flower business.

Now that he's back in Denver, it's easy. I see him more often than I don't.

"And if I had a best friend that looked like him, I'd be married to him."

"I don't think Jacob would appreciate that."

"Please. He is my best friend. That's why they say you should marry them."

I quirk a brow at him. "They say that? Who's they?"

"Doesn't matter. Look, I will help you get caught up before you go, because you're going. I won't take no for an answer."

"Ugh. You and Declan gang up on me too easily."

Leon drops a kiss to my cheek. "It's because we love you and want you to break out of your shell. Or…bud I should say."

"Har har. Aren't you funny with the flower puns."

"What can I say?" Leon bumps his shoulder into mine. "I'm funny. Now, get to work on these flowers. I need them done before you go to Vegas."

Ugh. There is no way that I'm getting out of this now. I've never been a big Vegas girl. Hell, a big partier for that matter. One too many drinks in college led to meeting Declan. I don't think I'll get that lucky again.

But he's my best friend, and I really can't say no to him. If he wants me in Vegas for a celebration of them winning, I'll be there.

Besides, it's Vegas. What's the worst that could happen?

Chapter Four

DECLAN

"This is where we're staying?" Alice drops her bag in the foyer of the hotel suite and spins to face me. "This is bigger than my apartment, Declan."

"I figured you'd be more comfortable if we each had our own room."

"I mean, yeah. But still. You didn't need to do this."

The two-bedroom suite is even bigger than it looked online. Striped carpet lines the room. A tacky gold mirror hangs on one wall with a TV directly across from it. A couch, complete with chaise and a small table behind it, fills the space. The windows beyond face the strip, the Eiffel Tower already lit up. There's a door to each bedroom, and a small kitchen with a wet bar behind me.

Alice disappears into one of the bedrooms as I grab the bottle of champagne resting in a bucket of ice on the counter. There's a congratulatory note sitting in front of it with two glasses. Popping the bottle, I fill each glass to the brim.

"I wanted to," I say as she returns to the living room.

"I would have been just fine in a regular room."

I shake my head and walk over to her. "I told you; this trip is on me. Otherwise you would have stayed at the hotel down the road in the smallest room they had."

She winces and takes the glass from my hand. "I would not."

"Really?" I quirk a brow at her. "I know you, Froggie. It's exactly what you would have done."

"Ugh, fine. You know me and my desire to not spend any money on extravagant things. Can we just toast to the weekend instead?"

I clink my glass against hers. "Cheers. Thanks for coming with me."

"You're welcome." Alice takes a demure sip of her champagne before walking over to the windows. "Did you ever think you'd be here?"

I move to stand next to her, taking in the Strip below us.

Lights from all the hotels.

People filling the sidewalks as they go to and from hotels trying to win.

"No. I never expected to get traded, but you know how things go."

I resigned myself to playing for the Knights, never even getting close to smelling the playoffs, let alone making them. First time I made it with the Black Diamonds and we won the whole damn thing. I don't know if I'll ever get used to that.

"I'm glad we get one more weekend to celebrate. You deserve it."

I wrap an arm around Alice's shoulders. "Thanks for coming with me. It'll be more fun with you here."

She laughs, warm and sweet. It's one of my favorite sounds. "Someone has to make sure you don't get into any trouble."

"I'm pretty sure you're going to be the one getting us in trouble."

"I doubt that." Alice gulps down her champagne before handing me the glass. "I'm going to go change for dinner. Be right back."

"Okay."

I set her empty glass down and go to do the same. I have no idea where the restaurant is—at this point, I'm just along for the ride.

Changing into a pair of dark jeans and a white button-up, I roll up the sleeves and add a spritz of cologne. It doesn't take much to finish up before I'm waiting on Alice. I pour myself another glass of bubbly while I wait. But when she comes out, I am not prepared for the sight that greets me.

"Holy shit. You look amazing."

I don't think I've ever seen Alice like this. It is not my best friend's usual look at all. Being away from her all these years, hanging out wasn't easy. With my hockey schedule and her working at the shop, it was hard to see one another. When we did, it was usually a T-shirt and jeans sort of meeting.

This? This little black dress leaves very little to the imagination.

"Really? It's the only thing I had at home." She brushes a hand over the fabric, looking down at herself.

Her hair is in a sleek, high ponytail. Her toes peep out of her shoes. I don't think I've ever seen Alice show this much skin.

My mouth is dry as I try to regain my senses from seeing her like this.

How is this my best friend?

"Yeah, you look great. I'm definitely going to have to keep you out of trouble tonight." A knock on the door sounds followed by voices. "Or maybe keep them out of trouble."

Striding over to the door, I open it and all the guys and their partners are standing outside.

"Ready for dinner?" Cash asks, his arm hanging at his side, loosely holding Piper's hand. "We don't want to be late."

"Oh my God, Alice!" Piper squeals as Alice comes up next to me, a purse now hanging from her shoulder. "You look great."

"Thank you."

Piper grabs her hand and the ladies walk down the long hall toward the elevators. The guys and I all hang back and follow.

The women are jabbering away as we're carried from the top floors to the bustling lobby. The sound of slot machines and cheers echo around the cavernous space. People are milling about the entrance to the hotel as Troy points out our ride for the evening.

A limo pulls around and the door is opened for us.

"Okay, this is pretty cool." I scoot inside and slide down the bench seat. Alice takes a spot next to me. "I don't know if I've ever been in a limo."

"Good thing you're paying for it then." Cash winks at me.

"You're a dick." I flip him off and grab the bottle of champagne that is already chilling. "I guess no champagne for you."

"Can I just say one thing as your GM and then I'm done?" Bexley asks, interrupting our conversation.

"Sure," Angie says, giving her a warm smile as the limo eases out into traffic.

"Please don't do anything that could get you arrested tonight." She holds her hands up. "That's all. I'm done."

Nick wraps an arm around her and presses a kiss to her temple.

"That was directed to you," Cash and I tell each other at the same time.

"Aww. It's so cute how much you love each other." Piper laughs from her seat next to Cash.

"That's the truth," Alice says.

She and Piper giggle and I can only shake my head at her. Because it's true. I love these guys, even if they can act immature at times.

Drinks are poured and excited chatter fills the tight space in the car. We pull up to a fancy restaurant farther down the strip before everyone clambers out of the car. Cash and Troy are ribbing one another and Nick is holding Bexley's hand as they walk in front of us.

"This is going to be a night to remember," Alice says, eyes wide as she looks up at the entrance to the building.

Yeah, this is going to be a night to remember.

Chapter Five

My entire body feels like a truck ran over me. I haven't felt like this since college. Since the night I met Declan and puked all over him. That was the last time I let my inhibitions go like that. I hate the feeling of being out of control.

I thanked my lucky stars that it was Declan I ran into that night and not some lecherous man. Things could have turned out much differently had I not bumped into him.

I groan. It's like a walrus took up residence on my head, it aches so bad. Turning my head to the side, I crack one eye open. Light spills in through windows.

It makes the pain in my head worse. I roll over, pulling the pillow with me. Until I run into a solid wall.

A solid wall of *muscle.*

Oh God.

I don't even want to look. Who is in bed next to me? The last thing I remember was the guys wanting to go to another bar and getting into the limo.

That was what…midnight?

The man next to me gives a grunt and the nerves leave me.

It's Declan.

But why am I in bed with Declan?

"Declan." I poke his side. "Declan. Wake up."

No response. Another snore. He is dead to the world.

"Declan," I hiss. "Come on. Get up."

This time, I shake him. That has him flipping over and peeking one eye open at me. "Why are you awake?"

"Because it feels like I've been run over by a truck and I need water."

"Why are you waking me up then?"

Declan moves onto his stomach and stuffs his arms under his pillow. His brown eyes close, shutting me out.

"The better question is why are you in my bed?"

"Your bed?" That has him popping up onto his elbows and staring down at me. His light brown hair flops into his eyes. "This is my room."

Before sitting up, I shove my arms under the comforter. *Thank God, I'm still dressed.*

Looking around the spacious room, Declan's suitcase is sitting on the bench at the end of the bed. His shirt that he was wearing last night is crumpled on the floor.

"I need water."

I slide out from under the comforters and scurry to the bathroom, slamming the door shut behind me. Staring at my reflection in the mirror, I'm a mess.

My hair, piled on top of my head, sticks out every which way. Mascara is smudged under my eyes. Pillow lines mark my face. "Oh God."

Grabbing the glass, I turn on the faucet and fill the glass up. I swallow the entire thing down. It makes me feel slightly more human.

Declan's mouthwash sits on the counter and I swig that down before washing my face.

Looking at myself again, I'm a bit more put together. My head on the other hand is another matter entirely.

Everything from last night is fuzzy. I remember dinner and the show. Going to two bars and that's it. I didn't think I had that much to drink, but maybe I did. We were celebrating, after all.

"You okay in there?" Declan calls out from the bedroom.

"I'm fine," I squeak out.

Opening the door, Declan is there, standing at the foot of the bed. His abs are on full display.

"Alice? You sure you're okay?" I don't know how long he's been standing in front of me. He snaps his fingers and that's when I notice it. The shiny glint of gold. *On his left hand.*

"Declan." I grab his hand and hold it in front of my face. "Holy shit."

"What the hell?"

My gaze goes to my own left hand. A matching band.

"What the fuck happened last night?" I shout.

"Do you not remember?"

"Would I be asking you if I knew?" I huff.

"I remember after the show we went to a few bars."

"How many were a few?"

Declan steps back, pacing in front of me. I'm distracted by the hard muscles rippling as he stands there. Thick thighs, with a light dusting of hair, have black boxers clinging to them.

How have I never noticed how attractive my best friend is? I mean, yes, logically I know he is. But I've never let myself *look*. No good would come from going down that road.

After the night we met, I spent all day with Declan, laughing and explaining my drunken thoughts to him. It solidified our friendship. I never wanted to do anything to mess it up.

Like get married?

"I remember you doing shots with Cash and that's about it."

"Ugh. I hate shots. Who made me do shots?"

That earns me a smile. "I'm pretty sure you wanted to do them."

"Then I was definitely drunk. I don't think I've done shots since…"

"The night we met?" Declan offers.

"Yeah."

"So we did shots and then decided to get married?"

"I have no idea." I shrug. "This is why I don't drink this much."

"Because you make bad decisions and marry your best friend?"

I cock a brow at him. "Yeah."

"Can I point out two things without you freaking out on me?" Declan asks.

"I mean…maybe."

That earns me a smile. "Fair. One—at least I'm not a stranger." He holds up a single finger below flipping up a second. "And two, based on you still being fully clothed, at least we didn't have sex."

I blow out a breath. "I did think of that."

I look down at my dress. Not the most comfortable thing to sleep in, but based on not remembering much of how we got to the hotel, I'd say it's a positive I'm clothed at all.

"Not that I wouldn't have rocked your world…"

I laugh. "So you think."

"Hey. I take offense to that."

I wave my hands in front of him. "This is not the conversation we need to be having right now."

"Look," Declan starts, "this is definitely not what we had planned for our trip."

"I know."

"We'll get it annulled. It should be fairly easy, right?"

"I think so? I've never actually had to get one."

"Hey, c'mere." Declan pulls me in for a hug, but I don't hug him back. He's still mostly naked. All these abs on display? I don't need to feel them. I don't need to feel his warmth seeping inside of me and making me feel better.

"Look. This will be a funny story we can laugh about in a few months, okay? I'll look and see what we need to do and get it taken care of."

"You will?"

"Yes."

That one word has me wrapping my arms around his waist. At least I'm in this mess with my best friend.

Okay, things really could be worse.

Chapter Six

The calendar alert dings on my phone from the passenger seat. I growl in annoyance as I turn on my blinker and press a code to get into the gated community.

It's been a long week. After coming home from Vegas, married to my best friend no less, I now have a family dinner to attend.

My presence was not requested. More like demanded.

It's one of the only ways to get me to come. To say I don't get along with my family is an understatement. It's always been this way.

My great-great-grandfather made his money during the gold rush in Colorado. We've had money ever since. I grew up with it, but hated the expectations placed on me. I never conformed to what my parents wanted.

Fancy parties with pretty dresses? I'd rather be playing outside in the dirt.

Pulling up to the ostentatious house, I, once again, press a code into the gate keypad to be let in.

The lawn around the half-circle drive is manicured to perfection. Not an inch of grass is out of place. Planters filled with pink Cosmos line the drive. Not the flowers I told them to plant. My mother said the gardener has a better grasp of what grows well in this climate.

Every time I see the pink blooms, I'm annoyed.

Parking my old car in front of the house, I grab the bouquet of flowers off the passenger seat and head inside.

Yellow chrysanthemums. It's the most passive-aggressive bouquet to bring to my family. Not only does my mother not like them because "they're cheap," but they signify sorrow and neglectfulness. Things I've always felt in this house.

Ringing the doorbell, I wait for them to answer.

"Alice. So happy that you could join us." Mom waves me inside, giving me an air kiss on each cheek. "How have you been?"

"Good. And you?"

Within seconds, the conversation is stilted. It's always been like this. I pass over the wrapped bouquet and receive a half smile.

"How kind of you. We're both doing just fine. Your father and I are having drinks in the lounge."

My heeled sandals slap against the herringbone-patterned wood floors. The two-story entryway is plated in gold with velvet wallpaper stuck to every surface.

It's gaudy and horrible. The lounge is even worse. Stiff sofas sit next to the empty fireplace. Built-in shelves, complete with an entire bar's worth of liquor, stand on both sides.

My father, still in a suit, is sitting in a black leather wing-backed chair overlooking the backyard.

"Alice." Dad gives me a clipped nod. "How is Declan?"

"Good. Happy to be back in Denver and to have won the championship."

I'm fine too; thanks for asking.

"Would you like a drink, Alice?" Mom asks.

Compared to her sweater set and pearls, I feel casual in my white blouse and plain black skirt. The tight collar itches around my neck, but I don't do anything to show my weakness. My mother will leap on it in a heartbeat if she catches wind of it.

"White wine, please."

Taking a seat on the red sofa, I cross my ankles and wait for my drink. Tension creeps into my shoulders at sitting in silence. I hate it.

Handing me the glass, she doesn't miss the opportunity to point out my posture. "You really need to sit up straight, dear."

"Yes, Mother."

I don't know how I'm not because my spine is a steel rod made entirely of the tension I feel toward these two. Dad walks back to his desk as my mom sits on the couch opposite me. The Persian rug might as well be an ocean between the two of us.

I take demure sips of my wine. Sloshing it back too quickly will earn me another scolding.

The room is quiet. The old grandfather clock ticks away in the corner.

"Must you tap your glass?" Mom sounds exasperated.

"Oh, sorry." I don't even realize I'm doing it.

"Don't be sorry. Don't do it," Dad tells me, standing and walking over to where we're sitting. "We called you over tonight to discuss a few things with you."

"Okay."

Nerves flutter in my belly. What in the world could they have to discuss with me? Aside from monthly dinners and a phone call from my father's secretary to set them up, that's about as much contact as I have with them.

It's for the best, really. I avoid this place at all costs.

"It's about your trust."

"My trust?" My heart falls. That's the only reason I'm still coming to our dinners. "What about it?"

"If you'd let me finish, I would tell you," my dad chides.

"Sorry." I take a cool sip of my wine.

"The lawyer was reviewing the stipulations since you are going to be coming into the money in a few months."

Eleven months and ten days to be exact. But who's counting?

"Right."

"What we weren't aware of is a marriage clause."

"Come again?" My mouth goes dry at their words. I couldn't possibly have heard them right.

"A requirement of the trust is for you to be married. In order to receive the payout, you will need to be married by your birthday next year."

"But why? Why didn't we know this before now?"

Dad scoffs. "I do not pretend to know why my father made the decisions that he did."

More like he wanted me to find a nice man, settle down, and become a copy-and-paste version of my mother.

That will never be me.

"And if I'm not married by then?"

My mother rolls her eyes. "It's really not that hard to understand, Alice. If you're not married, you won't receive the payout."

A lead weight settles in my gut. Ever since I learned about the trust when I turned twenty-one, it's all I've been wishing for. I can't stomach the idea that I won't get it because of a marriage clause.

My dream has always been to own my own flower

shop. Ever since I went with my mom to one when I was little while she was planning a gala for my father's office.

The colorful blooms. The paper-wrapped bouquets. The smells. I loved everything about it.

But owning a flower shop was not in the plans for my father. Jeffrey Burke's daughter would never do something so menial. His words, not mine.

The only acceptable job for me was to follow in his footsteps and take over the investment firm.

It's why my relationship with my parents has always been strained. I never lived up to their version of the perfect daughter.

Asking these two for money to open my own store? I'd be sent away with a stern look and told to never come back.

I've scrimped and saved over the years, but it was always to supplement what I would get with my trust.

It's so close, I can taste it.

My thirtieth birthday.

"Okay then." I gulp down the rest of my wine. It earns me a sidelong look from my mother.

But I don't care.

Because now that there's this added complication of having to be married, my head is spinning.

Married? If they had told me this a week ago, I would have curled up in the fetal position on the floor.

Now? Well, now, I might be able to overcome this little problem.

"That's it? That's all you have to say?" Mom asks.

"What else is there to say? Grandfather has some archaic idea that in order for me to inherit the money I'm promised, I have to be married."

"Alice, we've entertained your chosen…*profession* long enough," Dad snaps. "If you come work for me, you won't have to worry about getting married to inherit your trust. Money won't be an issue. What you make now is a drop in the bucket compared to what you would make working for me. Or even your trust."

"That's not what I want," I tell them, issuing a startling calm into my voice. Setting my empty wine glass on the end table, I stand. Just being in this house turns me into a moody teenager. I want to shout and rage and yell at them.

Why can't they accept me for me?

"You're not dating anyone, Alice. You can't conjure up a husband out of thin air. Why not work for your father and not have to worry about the trust at all?"

Of course my mother is on his side. She would never go against him. And what my father really wants? To control me by making sure I work for him because I don't have a husband to fulfill this silly clause.

Joke's on them since I have a husband.

"Well then, it's a good thing I'm married and this whole 'marriage stipulation' won't be a problem."

I ignore their shouts as I storm out of the house. I hate how they make me feel so small. Like my dreams aren't good enough for them. That *I'm* not good enough to be a Burke. So sue me, but I don't want to go into finance and make millions of dollars.

It was never what I wanted.

What I *do* want?

To own Enchanted Petals. And to do that, I'm somehow going to need to convince my best friend to stay married to me.

Chapter Seven

DECLAN

Got the papers from the lawyer

Does it seem complicated?

All pretty straightforward

I work late tomorrow night, so how about
the day after I come over and we can take a
look at everything?

Sounds good to me

Good

I'll bring dinner and we can discuss
everything then?

Okay

Discuss things? Not sure what there is to discuss. I thought it was going to be easy. Sign a few documents and boom, marriage annulled.

Locking my phone, I shove it in my pocket when I see Cash walking toward me.

"Thanks for coming to get a workout in with me," I tell him by way of greeting.

The arena is quiet. Now that we're firmly in the offseason, not many people are in this part of the building. Sure, the main office people are here, but I didn't see them when I came in.

"You're not the only one that goes a little stir-crazy."

Cash and I skate around the ice, sticks in hand. There are a few pucks on the ice, but we ignore them for now.

After everything that happened last week, I couldn't sit around my house and do nothing. I never thought I'd get myself into this situation.

Marrying Alice? Never did I think that would happen. I always thought I would be standing by her side as her man of honor when she got married. Standing beside her as her groom?

Nope, never.

"Have you recovered from Vegas yet?" Cash asks, grabbing a puck in the cradle of his stick and shooting it in my direction.

I debate wanting to tell Cash what happened. When Alice and I met up with everyone the next day in Vegas, we took the rings off and didn't tell anyone. If they weren't there, they didn't need to know. But honestly? It'd be easier if I told someone. At least to get their perspective, right?

"Define recovered..." I shoot the puck back toward him.

Cash skates over to me, sliding to a stop and covering

me with ice. "What do you mean? Did something happen?"

"I probably shouldn't be telling you this." I scrub a nervous hand over the back of my neck. Alice and I said we wouldn't tell anyone, but one person couldn't hurt, right? Besides, knowing her, she's probably already told Leon. Next to me, he's her closest friend.

"Now I have to know."

"Alice and I got married."

There's a beat of silence, and I feel like I can hear my heartbeat in the emptiness of the arena.

Until Cash bursts out laughing. "You mean you two actually went through with it? Holy shit. I didn't think you had the balls to do it."

"Maybe if you hadn't been egging me on," I fire back.

"Do you even remember what happened?" Cash cocks an eyebrow at me. "Because you and Alice were pretty wasted."

"Because of you." I flip him off. "I honestly thought you'd be the one getting hitched in Vegas by Elvis."

That causes more glee to spread across Cash's face. "Elvis did it? That makes it even better."

"I'm regretting telling you anything now."

"Sorry." Cash tries to stop laughing, but the smirk on his face tells me it's a losing battle. "I'll be cool."

"Fat chance of that happening."

"Dick."

"Ass."

"Honestly?" Cash starts, looking at me with a serious face. "I thought if anyone would do it, it'd be me and Piper, but I'm already planning our engagement."

"I guess only one of us could make a stupid decision in Vegas."

"Do you regret it?" he asks.

But before I can answer, the gate slams shut and we both turn to follow the sound.

"Hey guys." Troy skates out onto the ice, a smile firmly affixed on his face. "I thought I'd be the only one here today."

"Eh, figured it couldn't hurt to be on the ice for a bit."

"In other words, we were bored," Cash finishes.

"Yeah, same." Troy grabs one of the pucks and sends it over to me. "Did you hear what happened with Duncan?"

"What did that fucker do now?" Cash growls. If there's anyone that hates him, it's Cash. Seeing as how his girlfriend used to date him, it's warranted.

"Apparently he was caught at a party with multiple women, some of whom were married to other players in the league, and generally being a dick."

"Are you serious?" I groan. "Why is he such an asshole?"

"Do you want the long answer?" Cash asks. "Or how he just has a general lack of disrespect toward most people."

"I think you nailed it in one," Troy says.

"Is anything going to happen to him?" I ask.

"Nick didn't know. But according to Bex, the league is going to look at its player code of conduct."

"Really?" Ice slides down my stomach. Code of conduct? What if what happened in Vegas gets splashed across the sports headlines like Duncan's indiscretions? We were drunk. I don't want any drunken videos surfacing that could jeopardize my position with the team or Alice's future with Enchanted Petals.

"I don't know how he's still playing," Cash mutters. "He's a dick and his actions affect everyone. Not just him."

Troy nods. "Which is why the league is likely going to

start coming down on teams for the behavior of its players."

"Even harder," I confirm.

It's not like we don't already have a player code of conduct. It's not like we don't already have a player code of conduct, and having to conduct myself in a certain manner so I don't look like an entitled asshole has never been a problem for me. I love what I do and would never do anything to jeopardize it.

Cash eyes me and I know we're both thinking the same thing. Like getting drunk and marrying someone to only say *oops, just kidding* a few days later.

Fuck.

This is why it sucks to be in the public spotlight some days.

"Nick told me about it. I guess it's good to know people in high places." He laughs.

Considering Nick is dating the team GM, I bet it doesn't hurt. Not like he wouldn't have told the rest of us, but Troy is married to Nick's sister, and they see each other far more often than we do.

"Wonder when the memo will go out," Cash says, skating around us.

Troy shrugs. "It's not like we have to worry about anything."

"Well…" Cash voices.

"Cash!" I hiss.

"What's going on?" Troy asks.

Fuck me. So much for not telling anyone else.

"I—"

"Declan and Alice got married in Vegas," Cash answers for me.

"Hey!" I jab him with the butt of my hockey stick. "I was going to tell him."

"I didn't want you chickening out."

"You went through with it?" Troy asks. He turns his attention to Cash. "I didn't realize how many shots you were giving them."

"It wasn't that many," Cash defends. "Besides, they didn't have to take them."

"It was a celebration," I add. "We were having fun."

"Apparently a little too much fun," Troy says, smiling. "But yeah, it wouldn't be the best look for the team."

I groan. It's not like I was caught sleeping with married women—several at the same time by the sound of it. "Great. So instead of annulling the marriage, I have to ask Alice to stay married to me?"

Cash claps me on the shoulder. "Just smile at her. Who can say no to that smile?"

Troy rolls his eyes. "Okay, you might need to make more of a case than that."

"I figured."

To say she wasn't thrilled with this whole situation when we woke up the next morning is an understatement. Now, instead of signing papers tonight, I need to make this work. I mean, it's Alice, right? She's my best friend. We'd do anything for each other.

I only hope that extends to marriage.

Chapter Eight

I've been pacing the kitchen since the minute I left the team facilities. There is no way I'm going to convince Alice to stay married to me. She couldn't get away from me fast enough in the hotel room, like we were five years old and I had cooties.

Thanks to Duncan Fletcher—I seriously can't believe he's related to my old teammate Dax—I need Alice's help more than ever.

Instead of filling out the papers to start the annulment process tonight, this is going to be a different kind of conversation.

"Hey, Alice. I know you wanted to get this marriage annulled, but how about staying married to me instead?" Even saying it out loud to myself sounds ridiculous.

A crash in the entryway breaks me from my wayward thoughts.

Alice. Coming in like a tornado.

The ball of fury blows into the kitchen. A baseball hat, complete with the Enchanted Petals logo, hides her hair. A white T-shirt, knotted at the waist, hugs her chest.

Complete with black leggings and flip-flops, she looks relaxed, but I know she isn't.

Waves of anger are radiating off her.

"What's wrong, Alice?"

"What's *not* wrong?" she huffs as she sets down a brown paper bag on the counter. Based on the smell, I know it's my favorite empanadas.

I'm starving. I didn't eat enough before meeting Cash at the arena for our workout, and once Troy showed up, it turned into two hours on the ice.

"Do you mind filling me in, Froggie?"

Alice adjusts her cap. A sign of nerves. Huh. That's interesting. We're both nervous.

"We need to stay married," she blurts out.

"What?"

I couldn't have heard her right. There's no way. Staying married? Maybe this might solve my problem.

"Look, I know that's not what we agreed on, but I need your help."

I lean against the counter and fold my arms over my chest. "And this help requires staying married to you?"

"Yes." Alice nods. "Do you have anything to drink? This would go down better with a drink."

"Yeah."

Pushing off the marble island, I open the fridge and grab her bottle of wine. The one that I keep here for her.

Getting a glass from the kitchen cabinet, I give her a healthy pour. She gulps half of it down immediately.

"Okay, use your words, Alice." I clasp her wrist to stop her from finishing it off in one go.

"In order to get my trust fund, I need to be married."

"Since when?" I ask. "I thought you got it on your next birthday."

Alice shakes her head, walking over to the food and

starting to unpack the bag. "My grandfather apparently decided that in order to get it, I must be married. I'm sure my dad thinks that won't happen—and that I will decide to go work for the family business instead so I can earn enough money there to make up for not having the trust. But I don't want their money."

"I know."

"But if I want to get Enchanted Petals when Leon retires, I need it."

"Which leads us back to staying married."

Alice spins on her heel and looks at me. She looks resigned to this fact. "If you don't want to do it, you don't have to. I realize I'd be asking a lot of you and it's not fair, but—"

"Yes," I cut her off.

Alice is stunned into silence. A rare thing for her. "You can take your time and think about it."

"I don't need to think about it. If you need help, I'm there."

"But—"

I hold up a hand. "I might also have a reason for saying yes."

"Why?" Alice hops up onto the counter and sips on her drink.

I scrub a nervous hand over the back of my neck. "The league has been getting some bad press about players and their personal lives. Doing things that don't cast them in the best light. The league isn't happy about it."

"Okay."

"Basically, we've heard we are going to be held to an even higher standard. A player code of conduct, if you will."

Alice looks confused. "I thought the league already had that?"

I wiggle my head back and forth. "That's more on the ice. But now it's going off the ice, too."

I see when the lightbulb goes off. "And a quickie wedding in Vegas isn't the way to support this new initiative."

"Got it in one, Froggie."

"So you need to stay married to me."

I nod. "And you need to stay married to me."

There's a hard set in her shoulders. If Alice could get her trust fund any other way, I know she would. I'd give her the money myself, but she would never take it. All she has ever wanted was to own her own shop. Something she told me the day we met. Which is why I know her favorite flower and how she earned her nickname Froggie.

Because she called me a ranunculus when we met because I'm charming and it translates to little frog.

My sweet best friend. The one that got drunk and talked flowers with a complete stranger. One who never wants help from anyone and always insists on doing things herself.

"Why don't we eat and discuss the logistics?" I offer.

Alice smirks at me. "You're only hungry because you skated today."

"And? You got my favorite. How can you expect me to not want to eat?" I nod toward the bag next to her. "You know I love Maria's."

"What can I say?" She hands over a Styrofoam container. "I was trying to butter you up."

"Damn. I'm an easy target." I open the lid and breathe in the spicy scent of chorizo and peppers. I shovel half of it into my mouth in one bite. "You could get me to say yes to anything with these babies."

Alice smiles, taking a much smaller bite of her vegetarian one. "I'll be filing that away for the future."

"Okay, rules," I say around another mouthful. "It's safe to assume you already have a list?"

"I mean, nothing that I wrote down, but yes."

"Hit me." I set the container down on the granite counter next to me.

"You want them all?"

I nod. "Yes."

"Okay." She wipes her hands on her leggings. "We'll need to be seen in public. I'm thinking a few dates a month."

"Well, we already hang out as it is, so I can work with that."

"It will include PDA and holding hands." A slight blush creeps up her cheeks.

"Again, that won't be a chore."

Actually, it's an idea I very much like the thought of. Although now is not the time to be thinking about kissing Alice in public.

"We'll need to post on social media. Make it look like we're a real couple." She holds a finger up as she ticks off her list. "Lovey captions and all that."

"You might have to help with the captions, but done."

"I'll need to go to your games."

"You already come to them," I point out. "Does this mean you need to sit with the other wives?"

She nods. "Yes. It'll help in keeping up appearances."

"Okay. I'll make sure I get with team management and get you on the list."

Alice visibly swallows. "The last two you might have a harder time with."

"What are they?"

Now I wish I had the foresight to grab my own beer from the fridge. I don't want to let on that whatever she is thinking is making me nervous.

"I'll need to move in here."

"Really?"

"Yes. We can't be married and not live together."

Shit. I guess I really didn't think about that. "I mean, yeah, I guess so."

"I come with a lot of plants. I need room for them."

I look around my barren house. Moving to Denver and finding a place to live was my top priority. Getting settled was a different story.

The living room has a TV and couch. The kitchen? All necessary utensils. My bedroom? A bed and that's it.

Now that I think about it, it's pretty pathetic.

"Uhh, Froggie? Look around. You can have the entire house for your plants."

A spark lights up her face. "Actually, now that you mention it, your house needs furnishing. Maybe we can make that a date."

"Wow. You're taking your role as a wife very seriously."

"Speaking of my role as your wife," Alice starts. "No sleeping together."

"What?" That was something I never even entertained. I've *never* let myself go there with Alice. It's a line that can never be crossed. "I know that."

"I mean it." She points at me. "Not even sharing a bed. You have plenty of guest bedrooms in here that I can crash in."

I smirk at her. "And no sleeping with strangers while we're at it. If this is going to work, we can't be seen with other people."

"Considering I'm not dating anyone at the moment, not a problem."

"Thank God for that. Otherwise this marriage would be starting off on the wrong foot."

Alice buries her head in her hands. "God. I can't

believe the one time I throw my inhibitions to the wind, I end up married to you."

"Hey." I grab her hands and pull them away from her face. "At least it wasn't a complete stranger."

That earns me a smile. "I guess it could be worse."

"See? Bright side. Is that the end of your list?"

"Yes. Do you have anything to add?"

I shake my head. "I think you pretty much covered everything."

Alice hops down from the counter and stalks over to me. The resignation from earlier is gone. Now that I've agreed to this marriage, she seems more at ease.

She sticks her hand out. "Let's shake on it."

I take her proffered hand. I ignore how soft her hand feels in mine. How warm it is. The small calluses that have formed over the years of working with flowers.

"Deal."

Chapter Nine

"You know, you could have paid someone to do this," Cash grumbles to Declan.

"And miss your whining? Never."

"I am not paying people to help me move," I tell him as he passes over another box. "Not when it's something I can do on my own."

"Moving sucks," Declan whines. "I could have hired someone and gotten this done in a few hours for you."

I grab the box from him and pin him with a fierce stare. "They don't treat your belongings like they're your own. I don't want anything to break."

Walking into the open floor plan, boxes are strewn all over the floor. A few pots and pans are already out of the box but not in their new home.

"Please be careful with that one." I hurry over and grab the flower vase that is falling out of the box. It must have gotten jostled on the ride over.

"Sorry, Alice," Cash tells me. "Where do you want this box?"

I look around the living room. We're almost done

unpacking my car and Declan's with the things I needed most from my place.

I hold the pink vase with red hearts painted on it to my chest. It's my favorite and I don't want anything happening to it. "Umm, that one can go into the guest bedroom."

"Got it."

"How do you have this much stuff?" Declan groans, dropping one last box in the entryway.

"You realize how little I actually brought, right?"

I decided to pack the essentials. Since this marriage is supposed to be temporary, I didn't think I'd need to bring everything right away. Winter clothes? What's the point when we're in the middle of summer? I can get those later.

Declan looks around the house as Troy's wife, Angie, takes another box into the guest room. "Why is everything going in here?"

I roll my eyes. "Because Declan hasn't made space yet. As long as we get it inside today, I can work on this tomorrow."

She shrugs a shoulder and walks away.

"Really? That's what you're going with?" Declan asks.

"I thought it would be good to have an excuse ready. Besides, it's not like you've done anything."

"Because you're staying there and I didn't think I had to."

I shrug, dropping my forehead to his chest. "I feel like this is going to be a lot harder than we thought."

Declan rests his hands on my hips and I do my best to ignore the warmth it infuses inside of me. We posted yesterday about the two of us.

Every comment so far has been nothing but supportive. It was overwhelming, actually, to see just how invested people were.

Of course he got an earful from his mother that she

wasn't invited to the wedding when he called her. We decided to tell my parents in person at dinner in a few days.

Would it have been easier on the phone? Probably. But the lecture I would receive isn't one I want to deal with.

"It's going to be fine. It's day one. You're allowed to have a learning curve."

I look up at him. At his blue eyes that I know better than my own. "Yeah?"

"Of course, Froggie. Would I ever lie to you?"

I give him a smile. "No."

"Look how cute they are."

I startle, hitting the corner of my foot on an errant box and nearly toppling over if it weren't for Declan's strong hands.

Piper and Angie are across the room, hands clasped under their chins with hearts in their eyes as they look at the two of us. "I really don't know how you two managed to keep this under wraps for so long," Angie says.

"You two are in perfect sync. Like you were made for each other," Piper agrees. "You know, we should really get out of your hair. Let you break in the new house."

"What? No."

The blush that heats my cheeks likely makes me look like a tomato. "We said we'd get you pizza for helping."

Piper grabs Cash by the T-shirt and drags him out of the house. "We can get our own pizza."

"Yeah, you guys have fun." Angie winks at me as she pushes Troy out of the house.

"You really don't have to leave!" Declan calls out after them.

Car doors slam and it's no use. They're gone. Declan closes the door and surveys the damage done.

"Do you want to finish this tonight or wait until tomorrow?"

I cross my arms, giving him a duh look. "You know the answer to that."

"Ugh. I was hoping we could wait until tomorrow."

I shake my head. "You order the pizza and I will get started in my room while you knock out the boxes in here."

Now that everyone is gone, it's easier to make progress in here. Even if I didn't pack a lot, there are still things I wanted to bring.

Oversized prints of flowers to hang on the wall.

Framed pictures of me and Declan over the years.

A few books that I keep meaning to read but haven't gotten around to.

Pillows that I love and can't live without.

I easily put away all of my clothes in the dresser and take the laundry basket into the walk-in closet. Even though this is the guest room, it could still fit my entire studio.

I have never needed much space, but Declan has it in spades.

My room overlooks the backyard. A row of trees hides it from the houses beyond. A hot tub sits on one end of the flagstone patio and a barbecue is on the other.

"Kitchen's done. Want me to help in here?" Declan asks, walking into the room and throwing himself on the bed.

"Sure." I've made good progress, but there are a few miscellaneous boxes still to go. Shoes, knickknacks, makeup…things like that.

He takes the small box with my makeup and skincare products into the bathroom and starts putting them away. Not without comment, as he asks why I need so many things when I never wear that much to start with.

"No judgment," I call out to him. "I don't judge you for your jersey collection."

"Hey." He peeks his head out. "Those are collector items."

I point a picture frame at him before I set it on the dresser. One of the two of us at his first NHL game. "And what if I need that stuff? Leave it alone."

"Fine. I'll start on your shoes then."

"Thank you." I smile at him and finish unpacking my linens. Not that I'll need them because Declan has a fully furnished house, but I can't be without my blanket. Considering I'm always cold and Declan runs hot, I'm going to need it here.

"Umm, Froggie?" Declan's head pops out from the box he's unpacking. From the writing on the side, a box of shoes. "What's this?"

"Oh my God!" I fly across the bed and tackle him to get it out of his hand. "Close your eyes. You're not supposed to see that!"

My vibrator.

Not knowing what to do with it, I stuff it under the back of my shirt.

"Why is it in a box of shoes?"

The better question is who in the hell packed this box? I don't remember seeing it, but that was hours ago.

"Can we pretend like this never happened?"

Declan's face is a deep red, probably redder than mine. His eyes are still wide as he at the shoes that are now haphazardly spread across the floor.

"Is it safe to continue unpacking?"

I shake my head. "Go check on the pizza. I can finish in here."

There is no way in hell I am going to let Declan near another box. I want to wipe this day from my memory.

Him coming across my vibrator and looking at it like it has three heads? As if things weren't awkward enough that I'm now married to my best friend, he has to find my vibrator?

How do I face him after that?

Kill me now.

Chapter Ten

I wonder how long I can hide out in my room before it becomes weird. Something that's new with Alice.

Weirdness.

Had I not offered to help her unpack her shoes, I never would have discovered *it.*

Her vibrator.

Add that to the column of things I never needed to know about my best friend. Sure, I know she's dated over the years, but I never thought about that part of her relationships.

Just like I'm sure she's never thought about that in mine.

Glancing at the clock, I'm surprised to see it's pushing ten. I never sleep this late. And given that it's a Sunday, she's not at the shop since this is the one day a week it's closed.

Tugging a T-shirt on and a pair of shorts, I head out into the kitchen. The bitter smell of coffee perfumes the air.

Alice is sitting at the island with a cup in hand and her tablet in front of her.

"Hi."

She sputters, spilling coffee over the granite countertop.

"Oh, um, hi."

Based on the redness that spreads across her face, she's still not over what happened last night. Given how fast she sprinted out of here once the pizza came, I shouldn't be surprised.

"Mind if I have a cup?" I point toward the coffee pot.

"Sure. There's plenty."

"Thanks."

I lean against the counter and take in the house. Pillows that I used to see at Alice's studio are now on the living room couch. The flower book she loves is on the metal coffee table with a new set of coasters. The book-shelves that were pitifully decorated are now filled to the brim with pictures.

"Wait, did you do all of this today?" It wasn't like this last night.

Alice looks behind her before turning to me. "Yes. Declan, you have absolutely nothing to decorate with. The place needed a little sprucing up."

"Wow. It looks great."

Before I can go and look at each frame, the front door bursts open. There's only four people in the world who have the code. One is sitting here, and my cleaner isn't scheduled to come for another week.

Shit.

"Declan Andrew Paddack. You got married and didn't invite your parents?" My mother bursts inside in a whirl of anger and fury. "What is wrong with you?"

"Umm…"

She's a good head shorter than I am, but stalks over and points her finger in my face. "Honestly, Declan."

If her anger could make her hair redder, I wouldn't be surprised. It's not like I can tell her the truth, but would a white lie hurt? I don't think so. The only other time I lied to her was in high school when I broke curfew. She made sure it was the *last* time I lied.

"Why are you guys here?" I ask, deflecting from her previous question.

Mom walks past me as Dad gives me a hug. "She was bent out of shape yesterday, so we drove all the way here so she could say congratulations."

"Really?" I ask him. "Because I think she wants to bury me first."

"I still might!" she yells from where she is now embracing Alice. "Honestly, Alice, you picked him. Really? A man who can't even tell his mother before he gets married."

Alice looks at me, a contemplative look on her face. "Well, maybe he'll need to sleep on the couch for punishment."

"Ha!" Mom points a finger at my chest as I walk around her. "I guess Alice is a keeper."

"Well, if she's a keeper, why don't I make us all breakfast? I'm sure you're tired from your drive and want to chat with Alice."

Mom takes a seat at the counter and beams at me. "I guess I taught you something."

Pulling the carton of eggs and a package of bacon out of the fridge, I turn the stove on to start cooking.

The bacon sizzles causing a rumble from my stomach. It's already been a morning and I need sustenance.

"Tell me how he proposed," I hear Mom ask.

I drop the egg that I'm flipping midair. Fuck. Fuck,

fuck, fuck. This was not something the two of us discussed. Of course my mother would ask that.

Maybe if I focus on the pan in front of me, they won't notice that I'm there.

"Well, Mrs. Paddack—"

"Oh no, call me Kathleen. You're my daughter now. Please."

"Okay, Kathleen. It was a spur-of-the-moment thing, really. We didn't plan it, but Declan looked at me and told me how much he loved me, and has since the first day we met."

"What a romantic," Mom croons.

"Declan is a hard man to say no to, so when he said he wanted to get married, I said yes. I didn't even have to think about it. Even though he did say he wished you were there."

I peek over my shoulder to see Alice sipping her coffee. She looks my way and winks at me. What a fucking angel my best friend is.

"Oh, I should have known. My sweet boy."

"You know I wanted you there, but it was so fast," I tell them, turning around with the messiest plate of eggs ever in hand.

Mom waves me off like it's no big deal now. "Well, I'm happy I finally have a daughter with all these men around. We'll have to go out and celebrate tonight."

"Where are you staying?" I ask them.

Whatever goodwill Alice earned me is gone. The striking glare from my mom tells me I already know the answer.

"We are staying here. Why wouldn't we?"

"Because you always get a hotel when you come. You say it's a treat to not have to make the bed every day."

"And miss this time with you two? Never."

Dad sits quietly as he always does.

They are about as opposite as it gets. Mom, whose parents came here from Ireland to work, is the most outgoing, friendly person there is. When she went to school in Kansas, she met my dad. An engineering student, he is a bookworm and never talks. *Why add nonsense to a conversation if it's not needed,* he always says.

In looking at Alice, we're the same way. Where I'm outgoing and love hanging around people, Alice keeps her circle tight. I love being in the spotlight, and Alice is the definition of a wallflower.

If she hadn't puked all down the front of me that night in college, I don't know if we ever would have met.

"I'll get the guest room made up for you this afternoon. Maybe you can take a nap if you want, and I'll get us dinner reservations for tonight. How does that sound?"

"That sounds great."

"Declan, can I talk to you for a second?" Alice asks, nodding toward the living room. Mom and Dad are helping themselves to breakfast, so I follow her.

"What's wrong?"

"The guest room? Is someone else staying in there?"

"Shit." I scrub a hand over the back of my neck. "I completely forgot. No one is ever in there."

"What are we going to do?"

This close, I can see the panic in her eyes.

"It'll be fine. I'll tell them we need to wash the sheets and they won't know the difference."

"Declan. Your mom is going to see right through me. I can't lie to her."

"You think I like this? I hate lying to my parents."

"I'm sorry, I know you don't. But it's only for tonight right?" she asks. "Then they'll go home and I'll go back to my room."

I nod. "Right. Back to normal."

Or about as normal as it can get right now.

"We can do this." Alice reaches out and squeezes my hand. "We've gotten ourselves into worse situations than this."

"Like getting married?"

She laughs. "Yeah, like that. But I was thinking that time we tried to sneak into a concert in college and got caught by security."

"I only did it because you wanted to go," I correct. "I mean, who sneaks into a folk show?"

"Stop it." She smacks me. "You had fun."

"Until security got us. I'm lucky I didn't get kicked off the hockey team."

"Are you two going to come eat? Food is getting cold," Dad interrupts.

"We're coming," I answer.

"We've got this," Alice tells me before going back into the kitchen.

I guess if I have to fake a marriage with anyone, I'm glad it's her.

Chapter Eleven

"Wow. This is quite the restaurant." Mom looks around in awe.

"I thought you might want to try something different. It's new."

The dim sum, ramen, and dumplings restaurant is one of my favorites. Red lanterns hang down from the metal beams crisscrossing the ceiling. A window into the kitchen shows the chefs making the various dishes.

"How were you able to get a reservation on such short notice?" Dad asks, helping Mom with her seat.

I help Alice before taking my seat next to her. She looks beautiful in a black-and-white striped sundress with thin straps.

"Well, when I said my name, they got me in."

Dad gives me a quizzical stare. "Should you be using your name like that?"

"Relax, Aiden." Mom swats at him. "We're thankful you two were able to come out with us."

Alice smiles at her. "I'm glad you were able to come on a day I didn't work and we could spend the day together."

"Those bouquets you helped me make are just gorgeous. All my friends will be jealous when we get home."

"Well, you know when you get me started on flowers, I don't stop."

Dad took me for a round of golf while Alice took Mom to the flower market. It let them bond while doing something Alice loves.

"Maybe when you come out and visit us next, you can do a flower class for my wine club."

"I'd love to."

"Welcome. I'm Daisy and I'll be your server tonight. Can I get you anything to drink?" our waitress asks with a tablet in hand.

"Hi Daisy," Mom starts. "We're celebrating these two getting married, so we'll take a bottle of the house red."

"Four glasses?"

"Please," I tell her.

She nods before leaving us to the menus. Mom hands Dad his glasses and he takes them without looking. I study the two of them as they peruse the offerings.

I don't know if I've ever realized how in sync they are. Is this what marriage is like? You sense what the other person is going to be doing and when? Knowing someone better than you know yourself?

"Should we—"

"We'll get the beef pancake rolls," I tell Alice, finishing her sentence.

"Good. Those sound delicious."

I lean back and drape my arm across her chair. I hide my smile. I know we're technically married—even if only for the next year—but there is no one in my life I know better than Alice. No one knows me better than she does.

"Alright, here we are." The waitress appears with the

bottle of wine and four glasses. "Would anyone like to do a taste test?"

"No. It will only slow her down." Dad thumbs in Mom's direction. "You can go ahead and pour."

"Fantastic. Would you like to start with any shareables?"

"We'll do an order of the crab rangoon, your green beans, and the beef pancake rolls," I tell her.

"I'll get that in right away and let you enjoy your wine and will be back soon for your orders."

"She is so sweet," Mom gushes. "You know, in the past, I would have tried to set you up with her, but I think those days are behind us."

"Now, now, Kathleen." Dad pats her hand. "Why don't we toast the happy couple?"

"Yes, before you try and pawn *my husband* off on our unsuspecting waitress."

A feeling I've never felt rolls through me at hearing her call me her husband. I've had a few relationships here and there throughout the years, but none ever stuck. They hated my travel schedule, and I can't blame them.

Even if this is temporary, I belong to someone. I'm Alice's. I want to be hers.

She's always been the most important person in my life. If anything happened, she was my first call.

First NHL goal? I called Alice.

When I got traded? I called Alice.

Wanting someone by my side when we won the Cup? Alice.

It's always been her.

"Declan? Would you like some?" Alice nudges me in the side.

Somewhere between being lost in my thoughts and Alice nudging me, our appetizers came.

"Yes, thanks."

I take a crab rangoon and one of the pancakes before passing the plates around the table.

"Oh my God. These are amazing." Alice covers her mouth, chowing down on her crab rangoon. "This might be the best thing I've ever put in my mouth."

I lean back in my chair and quirk a brow at her. "Is that so?"

She looks confused until it dawns on her. "Stop it."

She swats at me, but I grab her palm and press a kiss to the center of her palm. "You make it too easy, Froggie."

"I don't know," Mom says. "These green beans are delicious."

I reach across the table and take a few to put on my plate, but can sense Alice's emotions at my move.

I've always been touchy-feely with her. It's second nature. I guess pretending to be in a real marriage to her is easier than I thought.

"Oh, you're right. These are delicious," Mom agrees. "Aiden, make sure you get a rangoon."

"I have one," he tells her, rather obviously.

I smile at the two of them going back and forth.

"Do you think we sound like that?" Alice asks, leaning close.

It's hard to read her eyes in the low light of the restaurant. Every blink of her eyes, those lashes kiss the top of her cheeks.

Red wine stains her lips.

"I—"

"Of course you two sound like this. You love each other," Mom interrupts.

"How can you hear us?" I whine, turning to face my mother.

"I have the hearing of a bat. Why do you think you could never sneak into the house?"

"Declan sneaking in? I can't imagine him breaking any rules." Alice laughs.

"Okay, we are not going to go down this road." I try to wave over the waitress, but Alice slaps my hand down.

"Oh, I want to hear all about high school Declan from your parents."

I groan, burying my face into my hands. Even after ordering our meals, my mom doesn't stop with the stories, and even my dad gets in on the act.

If there is an embarrassing story to tell, they have it ready to go.

"You tried to dress up as the school mascot?" Alice giggles, taking one last sip of wine as I pay the check. "I can't believe you never told me that."

"It wasn't my finest hour."

"Well, Kathleen, you are going to have to come back when you can bring photo albums next, because I want all the old baby photos of this cutie."

"And on that note, time to go," I cut Alice off.

After even one glass of wine, she can lose her filter. From the look on her face, she's not tipsy, but we don't need to keep going down that road.

"Oh, this has been wonderful. You know, I've always secretly hoped you two would get married," Mom tells us as we walk out.

"She has," Dad confirms.

"Wait, seriously?" That's the first I'm hearing of this.

"Who wouldn't want Alice as a daughter?" Mom says.

My parents have always loved my best friend, but this is news to me. Mom and Alice take the back seat as Dad and I take the front.

Their happy chatter carries us the entire way home.

"We're proud of you, son." Dad pats me on the back before I pull into the garage. "You've done well with your life, and that's all we've ever wanted for you."

"Thanks, Dad."

He is never one to heap on praise unnecessarily, so I take it when I can.

"Time for bed, you," Mom tells Dad. "Thank you both for such a wonderful night."

Alice hugs them both before heading to my room. Well, *our* room.

"Oh my God." I run smack into the back of Alice as she lets out a small gasp, and steady myself on her waist. "I forgot."

"Forgot what?" I sidestep her and grab the neck of my shirt and pull it over my head.

She looks behind her before turning back to me. "We have to share a bed."

"You know we've shared a bed before, right?"

"Yeah, but not as a married couple."

Toeing off my shoes, I kick them into the corner.

"It's not like it's going to be any different."

Alice crosses her arms and stares me down. Seems she's already taken a page from my mother's playbook, because it has me cowering. "It is going to be different."

"We'll deal with it. It's only for one night."

Alice ignores me and goes into the closet to change. Wanting to finish getting ready and be in bed before she's done, I brush my teeth and go to the bathroom.

When she comes out of the closet, she's in a skimpy pair of shorts and a loose fitting tee. I can barely look before she closes the bathroom door.

Fuck. Maybe sharing a bed isn't a good idea. One look at her and it's burned into my brain.

I throw the pillows off the bed and climb under the

duvet. Alice comes out of the bathroom and grabs them and puts them right back on the bed. Right in the middle of the bed.

"What are you doing?" I laugh. "You know we've shared a bed before, right?"

"Yes," she hisses. "But that was before we were married. I want you to keep all appendages on your side of the bed. No funny business."

I throw my hands up. "I'll keep everything on my side of the bed."

"You better."

Alice lies down and turns her back to me. I don't know if I've ever slept with so many pillows in a bed. Especially between me and another person. But if Alice needs it to make herself feel better, I'll deal with it.

One night. It's only for one night.

Maybe if I keep telling myself that, I'll believe it.

Chapter Twelve

"You look nice."

Alice walks out of her room wearing a white blouse, black pants, and a pair of low black heels. Her blonde hair, usually piled into a mess on top of her head, hangs around her shoulders with the slightest curl to it.

"Really? Nice enough to introduce my husband to my parents?" She fiddles with the buttons on the cuffs of her sleeves.

"You look like you're going to teach English at a prep school."

"Good. That means they will at least approve of what I'm wearing." That earns me a smile. "Not sure about the rest."

I can count on one hand the number of times I've met her parents. One finger, actually. I got a quick introduction one time in college, and I didn't need much more than that.

It's a wonder Alice turned out the way she did when she was a checkmark for her parents on a to-do list in life.

"I personally like you better in your overalls, but that's just me."

She smiles before grabbing her purse. "C'mon. Let's get this over with."

"Want to go out for drinks after?"

Alice nods as we head into the garage. "God, yes. Why can't my parents be more like yours?"

"Maybe if they were less intense, they'd be easier to get along with."

She sighs as she settles into the front seat, and I drive toward her parents' house. It's a short trip, given they live in this part of Denver.

No surprise they live in the bougiest neighborhood in the city.

"It's only going to be a few hours and then we'll be done, and I'll get you the biggest drink you can handle."

"And a few shots." She points a finger at me. "I'll need it."

We pull into their neighborhood, which puts mine to shame. At least I have neighbors in mine with kids riding bikes down the street.

Here? If there's a blade of grass out of place, someone will know.

Pulling into the half-moon circular drive of the last house—if you can call it a house—on the street, I put my Jeep in park.

There's windows and peaks on the entire front of the house. The gray stone house looks like it should be a ski resort in the mountains. Wood columns flank the front porch, where two chairs sit.

Not that I can picture either of her parents sitting outside enjoying a nice afternoon.

"Please don't hate me after this," Alice tells me, worrying her hands in front of her.

"Like I could ever hate you, Froggie."

"What if I tell you I don't cheer for the Black Diamonds?"

I feign a knife to the heart. "I'd be gutted and question your loyalty, but I wouldn't hate you."

"Good." Grabbing my hand, she leads us to the front door, where she rings the doorbell and we wait.

"Good evening." An honest-to-God butler answers the door. "Miss Alice. Your parents are waiting in the lounge for you."

"Thank you."

"Since when do your parents have a butler?" I ask, leaning closer to her ear.

"He usually isn't here when I come for dinner."

It feels like I've stepped into a museum. If I talk too loudly, I'll get shushed for disturbing the others viewing the ornate art.

Which just so happens to be the entryway of my best friend's house.

"Mom. Dad." Alice walks into the room and gives each of them an air kiss. Stilted at best. "Thank you for having us over for dinner."

"You really should have done something with your hair," Alice's mom says by way of greeting. "Let me give you my stylist's name so you can see her. She'd clean this right up for you."

"Maybe another time."

"Wallace. Celeste. It's nice to see you." At least I can greet them with the decency they aren't showing their daughter.

Alice squeezes my hand as I shake theirs.

"We hear you two got married. Alice was a bit abrupt about the whole situation." Her mom looks like there is a nasty smell under her nose. "Quite the news to drop on your parents and leave."

"Well—"

"It was a quick decision," I tell them. "If we'd taken more time to plan, we would have invited everyone."

Her dad's lips purse together. "I take it that means you didn't get a prenup?"

"No," Alice tells him. She takes a seat on the couch and I sit next to her. Every inch from our thighs to our shoulders touch.

If I can give her even an ounce of support like this, I will. I'll give her whatever she needs.

"I meant for Declan. Should this marriage not last, you'll want to make sure you protect your assets."

Oh for fuck's sake. He's more worried about me than his own daughter? He is a piece of work.

Being around her parents makes me appreciate my crazy parents. Sure, my mother is a bit on the overbearing side at times, and is a little wacky in the things she likes, but at least I know she loves me.

Not whatever sad excuse for feelings Alice's parents claim to have for her.

Draping an arm around her shoulders, I tug her close. She's as stiff as a board. Whether it's from the touching or being with her parents, I don't know, but she's not comfortable.

"Well, I don't plan on this marriage ending. Do you, Alice?"

"No."

"No one intends for a marriage to end in divorce, but you should have a plan to protect yourself," Wallace reiterates. "I'll get with my attorneys and see what we can figure out for you."

"Sounds good, Dad."

"Would either of you like something to drink before dinner?"

Her mom walks over to the liquor cabinet—more like a wall—and starts mixing drinks.

"I'll take a glass of wine," Alice says.

"Declan?"

"I'll take a water."

"I can make you a Manhattan if you'd like. It's what I'm drinking."

I shake my head. "No thanks. I'm driving."

Alice drops her hand on my knee. I don't know if it's to reinforce her strength or mine, but I have never met two people like Wallace and Celeste Burke.

Their daughter is the best person I know, and they're acting like she's the rug on the ground.

I take the proffered water and do my best to school my expression. No need for them to take their derision out on her.

She hands Alice her drink, and silence settles over the room. Alice sips on her wine as her mother looks around and her father does something on his phone.

Watching paint dry would be more interesting than this whole night.

"Sir. Dinner is ready in the dining room," the butler states as he comes back into the lounge.

Thank God. I don't know how much longer I could have sat in silence.

Four plates are sitting around a long, wooden table. Candlesticks line the table with a simple bouquet in the center. I don't know what kind of flower sits artfully in the vase but I'm sure Alice does.

An artfully arranged bowl of pasta, bread and a green salad await us.

"Our chef made quail tonight. I hope you enjoy."

"Thank you." I nod at Celeste, helping Alice with her chair and taking the seat next to hers. I drop my napkin across my lap and cut small pieces of…quail.

I've never had something so interesting in my life.

"Alice said you two got married while you were in Vegas?"

"We did."

I glance at Alice, not knowing what she told them because I was under the impression we were waiting until tonight to tell them. My guess is she thought it'd go easier over the phone. I don't want to say the wrong thing now and throw her under the bus.

"Your parents weren't there either?" Wallace tsks. "How can you consider that a real wedding if no loved ones were there? Honestly, Alice. I can't believe you embarrassed us like that. Our only daughter getting married without us."

She looks at her plate, pushing the peas around and around.

"They weren't, no," I tell him. "But it doesn't take away from our marriage or that it was, in fact, a real wedding."

I look him directly in the eye. I don't want him to treat his daughter like this. I hate seeing my best friend curl into herself.

"Again, Declan, you really need to think about a prenup—or I guess at this point, a postnup to protect your assets.

"With this happening so quickly, this is why you needed to protect your assets."

"Dad, can you please drop it? We're fine."

He tsks at her again, the conversation dropping to silence. The only noise in the room is the clinking of silver-ware against china.

"Alice, have you given any more thought to the finance position in my office?" Her dad sips his fancy cocktail.

She sighs.

"What's wrong with the position at Enchanted Petals?" I ask.

"She needs something more stable."

"Stable? I've worked there since I graduated," she clarifies. "Once Leon retires, I'll take over."

"Is it a stable industry? Finance—that's a good industry," her dad says once again.

"You know, we really should get going." I wipe my mouth, dropping the napkin next to the plate. I ate half the meal but that's it.

"And not stay for dessert?" Her mother looks horrified I would even suggest it.

"Sorry, but a last-minute event came up for the team that one of the guys can't attend—something about a sick kid—and they need me," I tell them. I really don't want to sit here and watch Alice cower to them a minute longer. I fucking hate it.

"Understandable." Her dad nods in agreement. "Work should always come first."

"Right."

"Dinner was lovely," Alice says, dropping her napkin next to her plate. It looks like she had two bites and was done.

"Thank you, Alice. We'll see you soon. And I'll text you my hairdresser's number. Just in case." Her mom gives her a hug as her dad says a quick goodbye before heading back to the lounge.

Alice grabs my hand and yanks me out of the house. She doesn't stop until she's leaning against the side of my Jeep.

"It feels like they like you more than they like me," she tells me.

"That's not true." I smile at her. "I don't even think they like themselves."

She snorts a laugh. "Well, at the very least my dad likes you more than me. He was so worried we're going to get divorced and that I'll take you for all your money."

"Well, we will get divorced, and if you want all my money, I'll give you whatever you need," I correct her.

Alice gives me a sad smile. "If all goes to plan, then I won't need your money."

"Fingers crossed."

I open her car door and let her get in. We've only been officially married a few weeks, but it feels weird to be talking about severing this tie to her.

I don't know what it's going to be like when this thing ends between us, but I only hope that we come out on the other side as friends.

Because if there's one thing I'm not willing to lose, it's Alice.

Chapter Thirteen

ALICE

"Enchanted Petals. Alice speaking. How can I help you today?" I cradle the phone between my ear and shoulder, popping stems of roses into a polka-dot vase to put out on the floor.

"Alice. It's Bexley Hart."

"Bexley. Hi." I straighten up. Why is the GM of the Black Diamonds calling me? Better yet, why is she calling the shop? "How can I help you?"

"Well, as I'm sure Declan has told you, our ring ceremony is in two weeks."

"He mentioned it, yes."

"Well, our florist who was doing the centerpieces backed out. She is pregnant and had to go on unexpected bed rest and can no longer handle the event. Anyway, I know this is last minute, but would you be able to help out and do it?"

"Me?"

"Yes," Bexley tells me. "Declan speaks very highly of your skill, and we would compensate you for the short notice, but we'd love it if you could do it. Something fresh and bright for the summer."

My mind is already spinning about gorgeous flowers that can be used in beautiful vases for the centerpieces.

Coral peonies. Ranunculus—just for Declan, of course. Lush garden roses. Hydrangeas. Dahlias. Cosmos. Add in some simple huck greenery and lush genestra, and it'll be a masterpiece.

"You'd really want us to do it?" I ask again.

"I'd love to be able to support one of my players' wives and have a local shop do it." Heat creeps over my cheeks. It's still weird to hear myself be called Declan's wife.

"We'd love to help you out."

"Fantastic." I hear her clap her hands over the line. "Is the contact email on your website still a good one for you?"

"It is."

"Great. I will get my assistant to send over the details to you. I look forward to seeing what you come up with."

"Thank you so much for this opportunity. I really appreciate it."

We end the call and nerves start to take over. Declan told me about the event. How every member of the staff is invited to receive their Stanley Cup Championship rings. It's a night that all the players have been looking forward to.

And we'll be doing the flowers.

"Leon!" I shout.

He's dashing out of the back office, a panicked look on his face. "What's wrong? Is everything okay?"

"Bexley Hart called and we are now doing the flowers for the Black Diamonds ring presentation dinner in two weeks."

I imagine my face looks much like his. "Two weeks? Do you know what we'll be doing?"

The tablet on the corner of the workbench dings. Grabbing it, I see the email and pull it up. "Umm, a lot."

I pass it over and watch as his eyes go wide. "Wow. We've got our work cut out for us. Three dozen center-pieces plus a few pieces for the stage?"

"We're going to have to work a lot of overtime to get this done."

Leon crosses his arms and looks at me. "You already have ideas, don't you?"

I smile at him. "You know I do."

He passes the tablet back. "You take the lead on this one."

"Really?"

He nods. "Get everything ordered and I'll help with assembly, but we all know how much you *love* the Black Diamonds."

I shake my head at him and start tapping away to our vendors' sites. If we're going to pull this off, I need to order flowers today. "I'm going to ignore you, because I need to start ordering flowers now."

Glancing at my phone, I have just enough time to get over to my favorite wholesaler before it closes.

Maybe I can even rope Declan into coming with me.

"Will you be okay manning the shop?"

"Honey, please. I can run this place with my eyes closed."

Locking the tablet, I press a kiss to his cheek and run into the back room to grab my things. "Thanks, Leon!"

ALICE

Want to go flower shopping with me?

DECLAN

When and where?

You're not going to ask why?

Do you want me to ask why?

Yes, but I'm going to tell you when I
see you

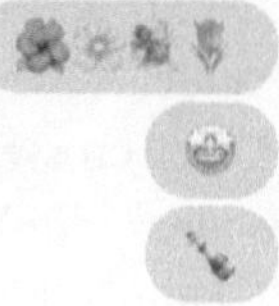

Not at all cryptic, Froggie

Text me the address

I FIRE off the address and grab my keys to head out. We've done big weddings in the past, but an event this size? It might be our biggest yet.

This could lead to a lot of great things for the shop. My mind is spinning with all the different arrangements I could do, but I keep coming back to my original idea.

Bright blooms to decorate each table to celebrate winning the Cup. Each one will be a masterpiece in floral form.

When I pull into the parking lot of an old warehouse outside the city, Declan is already waiting for me.

"Why are we here?"

Declan looks casual as ever in a black T-shirt, stretching across his broad chest, sunglasses covering his eyes, and a pair of running shorts and sneakers.

"Bexley Hart called."

"She did?"

"Yes. Enchanted Petals is doing the flowers for the ring

ceremony." I squeal in excitement. "Do you know what this means for us?"

"Alice. This is amazing. I'm so proud of you." Declan pulls me in for a bear hug, squeezing me tight. "I can't believe you get to do this."

"All because of you."

He shakes his head. "I'm sure she looked at your social media to see what all you do. It's all you, Froggie."

Linking my arm with his, I drag him inside. "Come on. We have some flowers to order."

The fragrant aroma of flowers greets us as we walk inside. It's cold in here, keeping everything fresh. Wren, my friend who works here, is waiting at the front desk.

"Alice. It's nice to see you," she greets me. "What are you looking for today?"

"Well, we've got a big event coming up in two weeks and I'm going to need everything you've got."

"Hit me. What are you doing?"

I cue up the tablet and show her the specs for the job. Telling her my idea, she nods along.

"Yes. This is brilliant. These are going to look amazing in this space. I can see them now."

Having her confirm everything I just told her has my pride swelling. My parents might not consider this a job, but I'm good at it.

No, great even.

"See what we have that you might want and I'll start work on orders."

"Thanks, Wren."

I wave at her as I pull Declan through aisles of flowers.

"So this is where you come to get flowers?" Declan asks, looking around.

Rows upon rows of shelves hold flowers in buckets.

Some are wrapped, ready to go out the door. I shiver as we pass under the AC vent keeping everything cool.

"One of the places. Usually I take them back to the shop every morning, but not today. We need them fresh."

"How long will all of this take to put together?" he asks, fingering one of the flowers on the shelf.

I smack his hand away. "Once they come in, it'll take a few days. I'll be pulling some long hours to get this done."

"I know you can do it."

I find the aisle I need, pulling out one of the ranunculus and examining it.

"Hey, that's our flower."

I beam at Declan. I love that he knows that.

"It is."

"Will I get to see the arrangements before everyone else?" he asks.

I shrug a shoulder and turn down another walkway. "No. You'll get to see them on the night of the ceremony."

"Including you?"

I laugh. "I'll see them before the ceremony. I have to put them together."

"I know, but I want to see them with you. I want you to come with me," Declan says.

I stop in my tracks. "To your ring ceremony? I assumed I would because we're married."

Declan grabs my hand and pulls me back into him. "I don't want you to come for that reason. I want you to come with me because you want to. On a date."

"A date?"

"Yes, Froggie. A date. What do you say?"

A real-life, actual date with my husband?

Butterflies swirl in my stomach. It feels like so much more than just a date. Like our relationship hangs in the balance on my answer.

I could say yes just to keep up appearances. But I don't want to. I want to say yes for my own reasons.

And that's exactly what I do.

"Yes."

Chapter Fourteen

For the last two weeks, I've barely seen Alice. If she wasn't at the shop provisioning supplies, she was buying flowers.

If I saw her, she was grabbing a quick bite before heading back to the shop.

I know what a big deal tonight is for her. Leon gave her complete control of tonight. Aside from one missing order of roses—which I heard about loudly at six in the morning—everything seems to have gone off without a hitch.

Adjusting the buttons on my cuffs, I slide into my jacket and give myself one final look in the mirror.

I decided on a navy suit with a light blue tie. Might be silly to wear Black Diamonds colors, but considering that my first season with them I won the Cup? I want a small nod to the team.

My hair is as good as it's going to get. Even if I wanted it to stay in place, it would flop right back into my eyes.

Spritzing on a bit of the cologne that Alice got me ages ago, I head into the living room to wait for her.

Pouring myself two fingers of bourbon—something I've picked up from the guys—I wait.

Did it feel weird to ask my wife on a date? Maybe.

But I didn't want her to come out of a sense of obligation. I didn't want her to set everything up and then leave.

I wanted her to say yes to tonight because she wanted to be there with me.

Ever since she moved in, things have been changing. I don't know if Alice feels them, but I want to spend all my time with her. Not that I didn't before, but things have shifted.

Changed.

There's a growing sense of attachment there that I don't want to fight.

The door to her bedroom opens and my jaw hits the floor.

Holy. Shit.

I don't think I've ever seen Alice look...so stunning before.

I've always known my best friend is beautiful, but seeing her like this? She's a bombshell. And couldn't be more Alice if she tried.

The one-shoulder, dark green dress flows out from her waist. On the strap sits an oversized fabric flower.

Her normally unruly hair is slicked back into a low bun. Her fingers fasten big gold earrings to her lobes.

"How do I look?" She stops and does a spin for me. Painted toenails peep out from the low heels she's wearing. "I wanted something I could move around in just in case there's a flower emergency."

"I…"

"What? Does it look bad?" She smooths a hand down over the skirt.

Gulping down the rest of my drink, I set it on the counter and walk over to her.

"You look gorgeous. You are going to be the most beautiful woman there tonight."

"Really?" A blush reddens her cheeks.

I press a kiss to said cheek and watch it darken even further. "I would never lie to you."

"You look quite handsome yourself." She brushes a piece of invisible lint off my jacket. I would know. I rolled the thing over a dozen times to make sure it was pristine for tonight.

I have to look good for my first ring ceremony.

"We'll make quite the pair tonight."

She smiles at me. "Hey. Before we go, I have a surprise for you."

"You do?"

Alice nods, holding her hand out to me. "C'mon. It's in the basement."

I follow behind her, taking in the way the dress flows around her. It's like it was made just for her. It teases at the hint of the curves that are usually hidden under a pair of overalls.

Why am I suddenly studying the way she moves? I shouldn't be.

Drawing to a stop, Alice points at the wall in front of us, and it takes me a minute to realize there's a new addition there.

It's my playoff jersey. The one with the patch on the front for the Stanley Cup finals.

"When did you find the time to do this?" On top of everything she's been doing for these past two weeks, she managed to get my jersey framed for me? "I can't believe you did this."

"Do you like it?" she asks.

"I fucking love it." I sweep her into my arms and breathe her in. "This is the best thing anyone has ever done for me."

"You deserve it."

Her arms squeeze me back and it's the best I've felt since hoisting that cup over my head. I shouldn't like this as much as I do. Shouldn't like the soft feel of Alice's curves under my hands. The way she fits perfectly against me.

This is all for show. For her to get what she needs and to keep me in the good graces of the league.

There's no one around to see us right now—holding one another for longer than necessary.

"Thanks, Froggie." I press a kiss to her forehead as I set her back down on the ground. "I love it."

"Good, I'm glad." She smiles up at me. "Now, let's go. I don't want to be late."

"WHAT DO YOU THINK?" Alice stands in front of me, the ballroom behind her, hands clasped beneath her chin.

"Holy shit. You did all of this?"

You would have no idea what's going on in here tonight based on how everything looks. I don't think I've ever been anywhere so…fancy.

The country club was rented out for the event. A large room with circular tables is spread out before us. On a small stage at the front of the room sits a clear podium, flanked by two large arrangements.

Every table is overflowing with bouquets. I couldn't tell you what half the flowers are called, but I know Alice did an amazing job.

"You like it?"

"It's incredible."

Grabbing her hand, I walk us over to one of the tables. Sitting in a low vase is a bouquet, surrounded by tealight candles and loose flower petals.

"I wanted to keep everything low so you could see the stage. I know there will be speeches, and I didn't want anyone not being able to see."

Alice is beaming, and pride threatens to burst out of me.

"You're amazing, you know that? Putting this together in two weeks? I can't believe it."

"Thank you, Declan. I wouldn't have gotten to do this if it weren't for you."

"You could have done this without me."

Looking at me, Alice rests her hands on my chest and kisses my cheek. Warmth spreads through me at the touch.

Fuck. That's new.

I should not be feeling these things for Alice.

Voices start to filter inside. Walking over to the bar, I grab us each a drink and go to find our table. Alice makes her way there and is talking with Piper and Angie.

"This place looks great," Cash tells me. "Alice did all of this?"

I nod. "She did."

"Damn. Maybe we should get her to do our wedding."

"I'll get you her number, when you finally get around to asking Piper to marry you."

"Are you excited for your first ring?" he asks.

"Fuck yeah. Hard to believe it's finally happening." It was what I dreamed about when I realized I was good at hockey and could make a career doing this.

Everyone mingles and sips on craft cocktails before dinner is served. A *steak* dinner. No expense has been spared tonight.

I'm loving every minute of this.

Before dessert is served, dishes are cleared and champagne flutes are brought out to everyone.

Along with the champagne, a large, black velvet box is set in front of each player, coach, and staff member.

The lights in the room go down and the stage lights up as Bexley steps up to the podium.

"When we started this season, going back-to-back was on my mind, but I didn't want to say anything. Doing that in this league is hard. In any sport. But you proved to me the kind of team you are." Bexley's gaze roams over the captivated audience. "This team is made of grit and perseverance. Getting to stand up here as your general manager is the honor of my lifetime. To see you grow as men and players? It's everything to me."

Nick is absolutely beaming at Bexley. Next to me, Alice has tears glistening in her eyes. Piper and Cash are whispering to one another, and Troy is absentmindedly running a hand up and down Angie's arm.

"We would not be here without every single person in this room. Every one of you contributed to this team. To our win. You represent this team and this city with pride. You make everyone proud to be a Black Diamonds fan." She grabs her champagne glass, and we all follow her lead. "Now, cheers to this team, and time to wear those rings proudly!"

I clink my glass with everyone at the table before swallowing down the gulp. Grabbing the velvet box, I crack it open.

And wow. Just wow.

"This is your ring?" Alice asks, peering over my shoulder as I open the box.

"Fuck, is it ever pretty."

Diamonds glint off every surface of the ring. Sapphires make up the logo of the Black Diamonds. Stanley Cup

Champions is etched in gold around the edge of the ring. My number is on one side with my last name, and the Cup on the other with the mountains behind it.

"How many diamonds do you think it's made of?" she asks.

"Almost three hundred," Nick interjects from next to me. He's staring at his own ring. His second since joining the team. "I may or may not have asked Bex about it. And that's not including the rest of the stones."

"Try it on," Alice tells me, her head now resting on my shoulder.

Popping it out of the box, I slide it onto my middle finger on my left hand.

Sitting next to my wedding band.

"Wow. That looks pretty good on you."

"Here. You try it on." I take it off and hold it out to her.

She slips it onto her finger. It dwarfs her hand. "I don't know if this is made for me."

"Good thing it was made for mine." I laugh.

She slides it back down my finger. "I wonder if this is what it was like when we got married."

"I wish I could remember."

Alice rests her elbow on the table and stares at me. "Me too. I bet it was a good wedding."

"Of course it was. It was ours."

"Hey." Cash claps me on the elbow. "Celebratory shots. Let's go."

I stand up, unbuttoning my jacket and draping it over the back of my chair.

"Take it easy," Alice tells me. "You know what happened last time."

"Got it, wifey." I wink at her and follow the boys to the bar.

The rest of the night is a happy blur. Drinks are flowing. Guys are sharing their favorite stories from the season.

The girls have taken Alice under their wing, and for that, I'm grateful. I love this family of guys that have adopted me into their circle and couldn't be happier they've done the same for Alice.

Closing the place down, we get a ride share home. Alice is quiet, staring out the window as the city passes us by.

As we left, people were taking leftover centerpieces home. She has one sitting in her lap. By the time we're pulling into the driveway, I'm ready to crash.

"Hey. Thank you for being there tonight." I hold open the door for Alice and take the flowers into the kitchen. I know tomorrow she'll work her magic to dry them out and save them.

She always does that after important events.

Alice drops her shoes in the entryway. Her smile is tired. "As far as first dates go, it was a pretty good one."

"You know, if a date goes well, you know how they end…" I trail off.

Her eyes go wide. She knows exactly what I'm thinking. "You really want that?"

"I thought I was pretty obvious about that." I step closer to her. The tips of my shoes touch her toes. "I want to kiss you, Alice."

"Declan." Her hand fists in my shirt. Whether to stop me or pull me closer, I don't know.

"What do you want, Alice? Because right now, I want you."

"I…I…" she trails off, biting into her bottom lip.

"I won't pressure you into anything you don't want to do, Alice. If you don't want to kiss me, we can forget this ever happened."

She doesn't say anything, but based on her searching eyes, she doesn't know what she wants.

"I think I've had too much champagne to give you an answer, Declan."

That's answer enough. At least for tonight.

"Think about it. Ball is in your court." Stepping out of her hold, I walk backward to my room. "Night, Froggie."

I leave her standing there, hoping she'll make the next move.

Maybe not tonight, but she knows.

I want my best friend. I only hope she wants me too.

Chapter Fifteen

ALICE

"Here you go. Have a wonderful day." I hand over a newly created bouquet to the woman at the counter.

"Thank you. These are absolutely stunning."

"I'm glad you like them."

"It was so cool the way you did the flowers for the Black Diamonds celebration."

"Really?"

"They were gorgeous. I knew I had to come get a bouquet from you."

"Well, thank you. I'm glad you could come out and get something you liked."

A furious blush creeps up my cheeks at her kind words. She smiles the whole way out of the store after I helped her put together something special for her daughter's birthday. Happy customers like that are why I love doing this.

It's nice to see that people recognized the hard work we put into the celebration and want to stop by.

I go back to sorting through this morning's flowers that Leon picked up, arranging them accordingly in the cooler for events and working on more bouquets to sell. A few knickknacks need restocking, keeping me busy most of the day.

Until Leon stops me. "Okay, what are your plans for tonight?"

"Going home to my husband?" I answer. It comes out as more of a question.

"Not tonight," he declares. "We're going to take you out to celebrate."

"Celebrate what?"

"Your big win. The store has been getting all sorts of buzz after the Black Diamonds championship celebration."

"Are we getting a lot of business from it?" I ask. Leon is in charge of booking the events, while I handle more of the storefront side of things.

"Yes. Business is doing great. I even got a call from a local magazine that wants to do a write-up on the store. Everyone wants us to do their events because we work with the Black Diamonds. Want the same vibes we gave our champions." His eyes sparkle. His passion is Enchanted Petals, as much as mine is. "So tonight we celebrate. Dinner. Drinks. Maybe dancing if we feel up to it."

"If we celebrate tonight, we are *not* doing shots," I clarify. "No way."

Because doing shots always seems to get me in trouble. At least where Declan is concerned.

"Party pooper. But you will have two drinks and after that, the number is up for debate."

I smile back at him. Leon is one of my closest friends and clearly knows me well. "That is agreeable."

"I love you, Alice. Thank you. Now, I'll finish up here if you want to go home and change."

I look down at my Enchanted Petals tee and torn-up

jeans. "You mean you don't think this is acceptable attire to wear out?"

"Jacob will have words to say about it—if you want to get him started."

"I won't."

Heading to the back room, I grab my things before leaving. I pull out my phone and call Declan. It rings and rings before going to voicemail.

"Hey. Leon wants to take me out to celebrate how successful the event was last week. I'm sure you're at practice, but I might see you at home before I leave. I'll see you tonight. Umm, bye."

Why was that the most awkward voicemail ever? It's not like I don't know how to have a conversation with him, so why am I being weird?

It's been like that since our almost-kiss the night of the championship dinner.

Ball is in your court.

I think about it the entire way home. All while getting ready and primping to go out as I change into something that Jacob would approve of.

High-waisted black jeans with a silk, leopard-print camisole top. Nothing over-the-top, but I feel confident in it.

I spritz on perfume before giving my hair one last fluff as my phone buzzes that my rideshare is here.

DECLAN

Have fun tonight

Let me know if you need a ride home

I SMILE at the text that comes through as I get into the car. It's just like him to offer to pick me up.

ALICE

I'll be okay

I don't want to get in the way of training

You could never get in the way, Froggie

THAT HAS ME SMILING. God, I wish I could talk to someone about this, but I can't. The person I would normally talk to about it is the one that is the reason I'm feeling this way. And I can't talk to Leon because as far as he knows, we're happily married.

Who knew deciding to make a move on your best friend would cause so much angst?

Traffic is crawling as we make our way back into the city. Even though it's a steamy summer day, people are out on the patios with beers in hand.

"Is here okay?" the driver asks.

Glancing up, I see the bar Leon sent the address for on the corner.

"Perfect. Thank you."

"Have a nice evening."

"Finally!" Jacob shouts when he spots me. "I thought we were going to have to drive out and pick you up to get you to come out with us."

"Stop it." I laugh, giving him a hug. "You know traffic sucks around this time."

"You knew she was coming," Leon says, rolling his eyes

at his husband. "Of course, if you'd wanted her here earlier, she could have come straight from work."

Jacob points at me. "Drinking in work attire is a no-no. That's just wrong."

"Hence why I went home to freshen up."

"You look wonderful." Jacob links his arm with mine as Leon gives our name to the host. The restaurant, in an old warehouse with exposed brick walls, has garage doors rolled up to the outdoor patio. Booths are packed to the brim with people. Following the stairs up, we're seated at a table on the rooftop—complete with old food trucks turned into bars to serve drinks for those up here. Large swathes of fabric blow in the breeze from the overhang we're seated under.

"How did you get a reservation here so fast?" I ask, dropping into my seat and taking my menu.

"I made it last week. I figured if I gave you time to think about it, you'd change your mind." Leon smiles at me before ordering the first round of drinks.

I wince. "Am I really that predictable?"

"You're a creature of comfort, honey," Leon says. "You like going to work and going home."

"Is something wrong with that?" Jacob asks.

"Not at all." Leon winks back. "But you and I get out. I used to worry about you, Alice."

"I am perfectly content with my life," I scoff. "There's nothing to worry about."

At least nothing I can tell them that I'm worried about.

Namely if I should cross the line with my husband.

"Hey, I said used to," Leon clarifies. "Now that you have your *husband* at home waiting, I'm not as worried."

"All she needed was some balance," Jacob says as drinks are dropped off.

I grab the lemon drop martini with the sugar rim and wait for the toast that I know is coming.

"Here's to Alice," Leon says. "For being a badass and putting our name out there and bringing in more business than I thought possible with one event."

"Cheers." I blush under his praise. "You know I love what I do."

"And it's why I love you," Leon says.

"Now why didn't that delicious husband of yours come out with us?" Jacob asks, sipping on his dirty martini.

"Practice." I sip on my drink, loving the sweet and sour taste. "The season is starting soon and I don't want anything to get in the way of another championship season."

"You know, I'm surprised we even see you as much as we do," Jacob says.

"What do you mean?" I lean back in my chair, crossing one leg over the other.

"Babe. You have the hottest man in the world at your house—"

"Excuse me," Leon interrupts.

"Hottest *straight* man," he clarifies. "Why in the world would you not climb him like a tree every chance you get?"

My head rolls back in laughter. "Did you not just say you were worried about me not having a life?"

"But not having a life and railing your husband are two very different things," Jacob says.

Leon pats his arm. "He meant thank you for coming out with us before going home to your husband."

"To climb him like a tree," Jacob finishes.

"If this is how you two are going to be all night, I might go well past my two-drink limit."

Jacob claps his hands. "I do love when five-drink Alice comes out. She always has the dish."

"Then I might stay closer to three-drink Alice. She keeps it together."

"You're no fun."

Our server comes by and takes our dinner order. It's the perfect night with friends spent laughing and talking about anything and everything. The kind of night you'll look back and remember because you love these people and the memories you've made together.

"I don't know about you,"—Jacob sucks down the last of his cocktail—"but I'm thinking we need to go do karaoke tonight."

"You know I'll never say no to belting the ballads by Celine." Leon flags down our server to get the check. "You up for it, Alice?"

"What was it you said?" I tap my chin with my finger. "Why am I not climbing him like a tree every chance I get?"

"That sounds much better than karaoke," Jacob says. "Maybe we should do that."

He grabs Leon by the hand and tugs him close as we descend the stairs. I pull up the rideshare app on my phone and request a car.

Leon presses a kiss to the top of his head as they wait with me. "After. Now that you've said it, I need to do some singing tonight."

The small car moves closer and closer on the screen before it pulls up in front of us. "You two have fun."

"Oh, we will." Leon waggles his eyebrows. "You have fun with that husband of yours."

"Stop it." I drop a kiss on each of their cheeks and climb into the waiting car. "I'll see you Monday."

"Bye, honey."

I rest my head on the headrest as we head home. Only

three drinks over the course of a few hours, but it's loosened my restraint.

Why shouldn't I have fun with my husband? We're only doing this for the next year. I'll get my inheritance to get the shop and Declan keeps his image with the team clean.

I never do anything that's *not* expected of me. I've always colored inside the lines and done what is asked of me.

Marrying Declan?

It's just about the craziest thing I've ever done in my life. So why not take that extra step with him?

Thanking the driver, I press the code into the front door lock and push it open.

I hesitate at Declan's door. If I do this, there's no going back. I want this. I can't stand being in Declan's orbit—moving around each other and having this weirdness between us—and not having him.

You can do this, Alice.

Giving myself one last pep talk, I crack open his door.

Chapter Sixteen

I know the minute Alice gets home. The front door clicks shut behind her. Her shoes clack against the floor as she walks into the kitchen before coming down the hall. I can hear her lingering outside my bedroom door.

Fuck. Come on, Alice. Get your ass in here. I want it more than anything.

Things have been…let's say tense these last few weeks. Ever since the celebration, we've been tiptoeing around each other. Well, Alice. Not me. It's like she's nervous I'm going to make a move on her. Like I said, the ball is in her court.

I'm not going to do anything unless she wants it. But fuck, it's taking everything I have to stay right where I am.

Light from the hall slips inside as the door cracks open.

"Declan? Are you awake?" she whispers.

"Yeah. Is everything okay?" I pop up onto my elbows, watching as she comes into my room and shuts the door behind her.

Soft footsteps pad into the room. "It's fine. I just…"

"Yeah?"

I sit up, watching as she comes around to my side of the bed and sits down.

"I thought about what you said after the party."

"And?" I lick my lips in anticipation of what she's going to say next.

"I want you to kiss me."

"Only kiss?"

I can make out her smile in the dark. "To start with."

"Then get over here, Alice."

She scoots toward me and the second she's close enough, I grab her and flip us around so she's under me.

Blonde hair spills out over my pillow. Her face has more makeup than I'm used to seeing. But God, does she ever look beautiful.

"What are you waiting for?" she eggs me on.

"I want to savor the moment."

"Can you savor after?"

I brush my thumb over her bottom lip. That full, perfect bottom lip that I can't wait to taste. To sink my teeth into.

"No. Because I'll never get to kiss you for *real* for the first time again."

"You're killing me, Dec."

I kiss the corner of her mouth. "Have you always been this impatient?"

"When I want you to kiss me? Yes."

I kiss the other side of her mouth, just to drive her crazy. Her cheek. The tip of her nose.

Anticipation ripples between us. I drag my free hand down her side. The soft material of her top bunches in my hand.

Holy fuck.

I am going to see Alice naked. Get all this soft, tender skin under my hands. Mark it as my own.

It's that thought that has me sealing my mouth over hers. A soft gasp escapes as her fingers thread in my hair.

Her lips are soft. So damn soft, so damn perfect, I could live here.

Sucking her bottom lip between mine, she tastes sweet. Like a sugared lemon, no doubt from her drink of choice.

"Declan."

The sound of her moan goes straight to my cock.

"So damn good, Froggie."

"More." Her fingers dig into my back, urging me on. "More, Declan."

"I know."

Kissing my way down her neck, I nip and suck on the tender skin there. Rocking back onto my heels, I gather the material of her camisole and push it up, revealing her soft stomach, before taking it all the way off. Her breasts are encased in a strapless bra, and I reach behind her to unfasten it and send it flying to the floor.

"Damn," I mutter.

My hands have a mind of their own, snaking up the soft skin of her stomach and brushing the underside of her breasts. She arches into my touch.

I swipe my thumb across the tender bud that causes her to dig her teeth into her bottom lip.

"Hurry up, Declan."

"There will be no rushing of this tonight, Alice."

Because I want to savor every damn minute of getting to be with her like this. Staring down at her chest, it's damn near perfect.

I lean over and tug one nipple between my teeth.

"Yes!" she shouts.

I lavish her with attention. I keep one hand on her breast while undoing the buttons of her jeans with the other.

But I don't go any farther. I toy with the hem of her underwear beneath, keeping my hand flat on her stomach. I turn my attention to her other nipple. Swirling my tongue around the tight bud, I blow a warm breath of air across it.

"Go lower," she says.

Her hand covers mine, trying to push it farther down, but I pull back, linking our hands together.

"I'm learning something new about you tonight," I say, staring down at her.

"What's that?" she whines.

"How impatient you are."

"And I'm learning just how much patience you have."

I nip at her ear. "Alice, I've been waiting weeks for this. A few more minutes isn't going to make any difference."

"If I say I'm sorry for making you wait, will you move it along?"

A cunning smile spreads across my face as I shake my head. "You can try, but I doubt it."

This time, I pull her jeans off so she's in only her underwear. A pink, sensible pair. Something so Alice, but sexy at the same time.

Her hands are in her hair, frustration rolling off her in waves.

"I'm going to have to start without you."

Grabbing her hand, I press a kiss to her palm. "No fucking way. You are not having fun without me tonight."

"I think you're the only one having fun right now."

"Teasing you?" I drag a knuckle over the wet spot on her underwear. "Fuck, yeah."

"See if I give you a blow job."

"Hmm. Is that on the table?"

My cock jumps in my sweats, totally on board with that idea. He can wait. Tonight, it's all about Alice and making her feel good. So damn good, she's going to want to keep doing this again and again.

"Not unless you do something—and *fast*."

Hooking a finger through her underwear, I tug them off of her. "Then why don't you sit on my face?"

"What?" That cuts through the lust-induced fog she's in.

"You heard me." I drink my fill of her pussy, glistening with need. "I want to eat you out while you sit on my face."

Lying on the bed next to her, I pat my chest.

"What if—"

"I'll be fine," I answer, knowing exactly what she's worried about. "Trust me."

Sitting up, Alice swings one leg over my body and wiggles her way up my chest. Grabbing her ass, I move her so her pussy is hovering over my mouth.

I press a kiss to the mound above her clit before moving lower. I slide a finger inside of her, moving her wetness around. Playing with the tight pucker of her ass.

She purrs. Fucking *purrs*. Oh, yeah. We're definitely going to revisit that someday. Not tonight.

I sink my tongue inside of her and pull her down so she's sitting on me. I can sense her hesitance at first, but the more I suck and draw out her pleasure, the more she gives herself over to me.

It's not long before she's riding my face while holding on to the headboard. She's lost in me. In the sensations I'm bringing out in her. Her head is thrown back in pleasure as my tongue moves between her pussy and her clit.

Her wetness coats my mouth. The delicious taste is almost too much to handle. I reach down and push a hand into my sweats to give myself a hard squeeze. There is no way I'm coming tonight unless I'm inside of Alice.

Fuck. Even that thought is almost enough to make me blow my load.

Using my free hand, I squeeze her hip, urging her on. I need her to come. I'm ready to bury myself deep inside her and feel her choke my dick to within an inch of his life.

"Oh…Declan."

Glancing up, her blue eyes are locked on me. It only takes a few more licks before she's exploding on my tongue.

Yessss.

I moan against her as I lap up every drop of her release, willing myself not to follow her over the cliff.

Because getting to taste Alice for the first time?

Nothing will ever top this.

Moving her off of me, I lay her on the bed next to me. She is blissed out and sexy as hell like this. A blush creeps up over her chest.

"How do you feel?"

She turns to me with a happy smile on her face. "Incredible."

I press a kiss to her neck before hopping off the bed and shucking off my sweats. "I'm about to make you feel even better."

"I don't know if you can top that."

"Is that a challenge?" I ask.

Her eyes rake over me, locking on to where I'm stroking myself.

"No."

"It's not?"

"I'm learning if I'm impatient, then you won't hurry up."

Crawling onto the bed, I rest my weight over her. Her legs come around my hips to wrap around me.

Her mouth captures mine in a lazy kiss. It has me sliding my cock along her wet pussy.

"Declan, please."

Fuck. I don't think there is a better sound than hearing Alice beg for me.

"Condom?" I ask, dropping my hands on either side of her head.

She shakes her head. "No. All my tests are negative and I have an IUD."

"Mine too."

Reaching between us, she grabs my dick and lines it up. I slide through her fist and into her sweet, warm pussy.

"Fuck," I growl. "Fuck."

Her inner walls are fluttering as I push all the way inside.

"Declan."

I kiss every inch of skin I can. "So damn good, Froggie."

My moves are slow and methodical. Fire flashes through my veins with each thrust, causing Alice's nails to dig into my back.

"I love how you're making me feel," she whispers.

I drop my forehead to hers, watching as I pump in and out. The way she sucks me in is like I was made for her and her only.

"I'm going to come, Alice. Fuck. You feel too damn good not to come inside of you."

"I'm with you, Declan. I'm…"

She doesn't get another word out as she comes again.

"Yesss," I hiss. I move harder and faster, needing to follow her over. It doesn't take but a few more pumps before I'm exploding. "Fuck!"

We hold each other through our orgasms before I pull out of her. Cum leaks out of her and damn, if I don't love that visual.

Marking *my wife* as my own.

Our bodies are sticky as I collapse on top of her. Warm lips kiss my neck and shoulder as my breath ghosts across her chest.

"Wow," she whispers.

"Yeah."

I make no effort to move, loving the feel of being wrapped up in her arms. Instead, I pull the sheet over us, needing sleep before we go another round.

"I'm sorry I made you wait so long," she says.

"Why's that?"

"Because that was amazing."

I press a kiss to her chest.

"There's a lot more where that came from."

Chapter Seventeen

Stretching my body, a delicious ache rolls through me. Memories of last night swarm me like a tidal wave. Of everything that Declan and I did. I don't know why I was so worried. I've never experienced anything so pleasurable in my entire life. I mean, I knew Declan would be amazing, but wow. I never expected *that*.

Reaching out next to me, I confirm the bed is empty. Given that I can hear noise coming from the kitchen, I know where he is.

It's still dark in here, the curtains and blinds drawn. Since I don't have to go to Enchanted Petals today, I'm in no rush to get up.

I'd rather Declan come back to bed so we can have a repeat of last night.

When the door creaks open and he walks in—in those same gray sweatpants—holding a tray, happiness warms my body.

"Morning, Froggie."

"Morning."

I sit up, covering my chest with the sheet.

"I thought you could use some breakfast."

"Oh, yeah?" I rub a hand over my tired eyes. "Is this what I can expect every time we have sex?"

He grabs a piece of bacon and munches down on it. "I mean, if you want it, I can make it happen."

"I don't need it," I say, grabbing a mug of coffee. "I do appreciate it."

"How are you feeling?" he asks, rubbing my calf through the soft sheet.

"Honestly? I'm—"

"I mean, yeah, I'd prefer you're honest," he interrupts. "I don't want you to lie."

"Why would I lie?"

"In case it was the worst sex of your life."

"Declan." I laugh. "Do you think I could have faked those orgasms you gave me? Multiple, I might add?"

"That was our first time having sex, Froggie. For all I know, you could be a master faker."

Setting my coffee mug on the nightstand, I link my fingers behind Declan's neck and pull him close. "I can assure you—*honestly*—that there was no faking. I have never felt better."

"Good." He kisses me. Soft, sweet, and way too quick for my liking.

That same heat from last night makes butterflies explode low in my belly. Has my body always reacted like this to Declan and I just pushed the feelings aside without realizing it?

Real, legitimate feelings for him. My best friend.

It's uncharted territory for me.

Before I can let my mind wander too far, Declan pulls me back.

"What changed your mind last night?"

"It was Leon."

"Leon? Really?"

I grab one of the croissants and tear off a corner, popping the fluffy pastry in my mouth.

"He asked why I was out with him and Jacob instead of at home with my sexy husband."

He smiles back at me. "Leon does have good taste."

"He does."

"Remind me to thank him later."

I roll my eyes. "You're going to tell my boss thanks for convincing your wife to have sex with you? When we're supposed to be having sex this whole time?"

"Okay, fine," he says, "but I should at least send him a fruit basket or something."

"No fruit basket is needed, Declan."

"It's not like I can send him flowers." He tears off the other half of the pastry and eats it.

"Or, you know, just don't say anything." I shrug my shoulder. The sheet slips lower, exposing the top of my chest.

"I could be convinced not to say anything."

"Oh, yeah?"

Leaning back against the headboard, the soft cotton pools around my waist.

"Yeah."

Declan latches onto my nipple. "Oh shit, that feels amazing."

"I love how responsive you are to me."

"It's so good, Dec."

His mouth devours my breasts, showering them in attention. It's the best way to wake up. Even better than coffee.

"You feeling good enough to do it again?" he asks.

Pushing him back onto the bed, I pull his sweats down.

"Remember what I said last night?" I drag a finger along the underside of his dick, watching as it jumps.

"Yeah."

"Then let me make you feel good before you fuck me again."

"Fuck."

I seal my mouth over the head of his cock, lapping up the precum leaking out. He pushes my hair out of my face as I take more of him inside.

His dick is the perfect size. Swallowing as much of him as I can, I use my other hand to play with his balls.

Releasing him, I lick a path back up before swirling my tongue through the slit.

"So good, Declan."

He tilts my chin up to face him. "Do you realize how good you look with my cock in your mouth?"

"Want to know what would be even better?"

"What's that?"

"If we spend all day doing this."

Declan rests his hands behind his hand, a cocky grin now on his face. "If you really want."

I nod, lazily moving my hand up and down his cock. "I mean, there are a lot of places we can christen in this house."

"I kind of like that idea. You and me having a sex-filled day."

"Like a belated wedding celebration."

"I'll give you a belated wedding celebration."

"Wait, are we talking about a real one?" I ask. Now I'm confused.

"Hell, if you want to celebrate our wedding, us moving in together, we can do it. But right now, the only thing I want to do is to have our own celebration. I want this pussy of yours again."

"Mmm." I suck his cock back down into my mouth.

"It seems you like that idea," he says.

Popping off him, I wipe my mouth and straddle his hips. "Is this what you want?"

I roll my pussy up and down his dick.

"Fuck. I could get off just like this." Declan's fingers dig into my hips.

"You're not the only one."

He slaps my ass, heat simmering through me. "Then get going."

Resting my hands on my chest, I ignore him, continuing my ministrations. "I think I deserve at least one orgasm before you come inside me again."

"Fuck," he bites out. "I like this side of you, Froggie."

"Oh, yeah? What side is that?"

"The side that takes what you want."

Each glide of his cock through my wet pussy sends fire racing through me. "You make me feel so damn good, Dec."

"Come on my cock so I can come inside you then. You're killing me."

When the tip of his dick brushes past my clit, I can't hold it together any longer. I combust.

"Declan!" I shout.

"Fuck, so good, Alice." His fingers bruise my hips as he keeps rocking me over his hard length as I come and come.

It feels endless, stars bursting behind my eyes as lust travels through my body. The vibrations rocketing inside me are like nothing I've ever felt before. Holy shit. This is probably the greatest orgasm I've ever had in my life, and I know being with Declan like this, it's only just the beginning.

"How do you make me feel so good?" I whisper.

"Not as good as you make me feel."

A soft smile plays on Declan's face as he looks up at me. It makes my heart bang around in my chest.

It stirs up a lot of feelings. A lot of feelings that I shouldn't be having for my husband. But I don't want to think about that right now.

I only want to bask in how good this man is making me feel.

Reaching between us, I line Declan up and slowly sink down on him. The stretch is delicious as I dig my nails into his chest.

He reaches up and strums my clit as I swivel my hips, adjusting to his size.

"That feels incredible."

My moves are slow and measured as I lift off him and move back down. He hits somewhere inside me even deeper than last night.

"You're driving me crazy," he grinds out. "Faster."

"No." I shake my head. "This feels perfect."

"I know I shouldn't complain because I've been wanting you so much."

"Yeah?" I drop my hands onto either side of his head, not stopping the movement of my hips.

"I've wanted you so badly. Fuck. I know the ball was in your court, but damn, Alice. The wait was killing me."

"I guess that means we'll have to make up for lost time."

Declan pulls me closer, mouths connecting as our bodies do the talking. I get swept up in this man. Each shift of my hips pushes me that much closer to tipping over the edge.

And when I do?

Declan comes with me, making it even better than last night. Feeling his cum inside me is like nothing I've ever experienced. I've never gone bare before, but I can't imagine doing it with anyone else.

"Holy shit." I pull off of him and collapse next to him.

He pulls me into his side, his softening dick pressing into my back.

"You got that right."

"How is each orgasm better than the last?"

"Is that a challenge?" he asks, tracing a pattern into my stomach.

"I mean, no, but if you want it to be, I won't mind you trying."

"Good. Then you should eat breakfast."

"Oh, yeah?" I huff out a breath.

"Yeah. Because if I plan on making each one better than the last, we'll be doing this all day long."

Chapter Eighteen

"Someone looks happy," Leon says.

"Stop it."

I trim a bundle of roses, wrapping them in butcher paper before moving them to cold storage.

"Just saying…you look happier than I've seen you look in a long time."

"Could be because you gave me Saturday off."

With the store closed on Sundays, it's the only day off I take during the week. And before Declan and I got married, I used to come in to get ahead on orders.

This last weekend? It was the first time off I've taken in a long time. Well, at least since Vegas.

"Or it could be because you spent the weekend in bed with that husband of yours."

My cheeks burn hot. "You can't say things like that at work."

"It's never bothered you before."

"Yeah, because we were talking about *your* sex life. Not mine."

He elbows me in the side, grabbing the empty bucket

off the work bench. "It's more exciting when it's yours because you never have any fun."

"Hey!" I scoff. "I have fun."

"Yeah, but not the sexy kind of fun. You're way more mellow today."

"Am I?"

I toy with the end of my braid.

"Yes. Clearly sex with your husband is good for you."

"Okay." I point a finger at him. "You have got to stop saying that. What if a customer walks in?"

"My store, my rules."

"See if I stick around."

He shakes his head at me. "As if you'll go anywhere else. Besides, this place will hopefully be yours this time next year."

"When I will implement a no-sex-talk-at-the-shop rule." I laugh.

"Good luck!" he singsongs as he heads to the back to grab more flowers.

The whole reason I'm so happy *is* because of Declan and the weekend we spent together. I hated leaving him this morning, but between my job and him going for a workout session with the guys, our time was cut short.

I can't wait to get to go home to him. Leon's reminder that this place could be mine next year is why Declan and I are doing this.

Not that I need the reminder, but Enchanted Petals is what I've always wanted. Ever since Leon gave me the job, I've loved this place. More than anything else in the world.

So what if I was a workaholic? I have a fun life, regardless of what Leon thinks. But now there's the added element of my husband. And not just my husband that I'm staying married to in order to buy this place.

No, there's my husband whom I very much enjoy having sex with.

I don't think of the added complications. There will come a time for that. Once heat on the league has died down around the personal lives of players, people will forget about our announcement. I'll get my shop, and we can quietly divorce.

Why does that thought make me sick to my stomach already?

"Hey, Froggie."

The door jingles, startling me out of my thoughts, and in walks my husband. Holy shit.

He is so damn sexy, it hurts.

How did it take me so long to notice this about him?

"What are you doing here?" I glance down at my watch. "I thought you were working out with the guys."

"I am. Well, did. I thought I'd stop by on my way home."

"Aren't you a charmer?" Leon bursts out of the back room, wiggling his fingers in greeting to Declan. "I wish my husband would stop by more."

"It's that newlywed bliss," he says, hopping up to sit on the workbench. "Leon, I owe you a thank you."

"For what?" His gaze flits back and forth between the two of us.

"Declan!" I hiss.

He better not be going where I think he's going with this.

"For giving Alice the day off this weekend. I appreciate it."

Leon waves him off. "Alice works too hard. She needs to take more time off."

I blow out a breath, leaning against the table where

Declan sits. "I keep trying to tell her that, but she won't listen."

"Because we're busy," I say, trying to go back to work, but to no avail. "Someone has to take their job seriously."

"Ouch." Leon feigns hurt. "I happen to take my job very seriously. But I also have something called work-life balance."

"Froggie is still learning about that," Declan says, pressing a kiss to the crown of my head. "It's why we love her."

Leon bats his eyes at us. "You two are seriously the cutest."

"Thanks," Declan says. "While you're here, we're going to be having people over on Friday night to celebrate the wedding."

"We are?" I ask. This is the first I'm hearing about this.

"Remember? We talked about it this weekend."

"I remember a very different conversation."

Warmth blooms up my cheeks. Although, I'm pretty sure that a dozen killer orgasms will push all rational thought from your head.

"I mentioned it to the guys today, and they were all about it. They'll be over Friday night, so you and Jacob need to come," Declan says.

"Sounds great." Leon pulls his phone out of his apron. "I'll put it in the calendar now."

"Do you think you can give your best employee the afternoon off?"

"Best?" Leon laughs. "Alice has been employee of the month ever since she started, and I'm including myself in that. She can have as many afternoons off as she wants."

"Good. I've got it all planned, so she doesn't need to do anything."

"Can I at least bring the flowers?" I ask.

"No," they both answer.

"I will take care of that," Leon says. "I do know a thing or two about what you like."

"Ugh. Fine."

"Don't sound so excited, Froggie."

"I don't like when the two of you gang up on me."

Declan presses a kiss to my lips. "It's only because we love you."

"Yeah, yeah." I roll my eyes at both of them. "Would you two let me get back to work so I can get some things done?"

Declan hops off the counter. "I'll see you at home?"

"I'll be home at my usual time."

He wags his brows at me. "Don't be late. I want a replay of this weekend."

It's that promise that carries me through the rest of the day.

Going home to my husband? I think I can find some work-life balance for that.

Chapter Nineteen

DECLAN

"We really should have told Leon to come early," Alice says, wiping her hands on the towel, then rearranging the food. Again.

"It's our friends, Froggie. We don't *have* to impress them."

"But this is the first time they're coming to your house when we're married."

I quirk a brow at her. "You mean *our* house?"

"Yes, our house."

I grab a carrot and pop it into my mouth. "You need to get used to that. You don't want to blow our cover."

"Sorry, I'm nervous. I want everything to be perfect."

"Trust me." I pull her against me. "It's going to be fine. The guys will be happy we're feeding them."

"Okay."

"Let me make you a drink to help you settle down."

Brushing a kiss against her forehead, I grab the vodka and lemons from the refrigerator to make her usual drink.

I shouldn't be surprised that she's nervous for tonight.

She wants everything to be perfect. No doubt a trait drilled into her by her parents.

She pulls the glasses from the cabinet and gets ice out as I pour a shot of vodka into her glass before mixing my old-fashioned.

The two of us work in perfect sync together. It's like we've always been doing this. Hell, even if we weren't married we'd be doing this. It's a dance we've been doing ever since college.

I like the fact that I get to be doing it now with *my wife*.

Giving both drinks a final stir, I hand Alice hers. "Cheers to the Paddacks."

"Cheers."

She sips on her drink, but before she gets far, I pull her in for a kiss.

"Are you trying to get me all flustered?"

"I was hoping that and the drink would calm you down."

"It's making me want to do other things that we definitely don't have time for."

"Froggie, you're killing me."

"It's a good thing you love me." She winks at me.

"Probably why I married you too."

"That and several bottles of champagne."

I wish her words didn't sting as much as they did. Did I plan on waking up in Vegas married to my best friend? No, but I find that I'm liking the idea of being married to her more and more.

Expiration on this thing be damned.

The doorbell rings, echoing around the house. Whatever ease Alice was just feeling, she appears flustered again.

"I didn't expect them to be right on time."

"No one wants extra drills if we're late for practice."

"How do I look?" she asks, doing a little spin.

In a pair of wide-leg jeans and a black bodysuit, she looks as sexy as ever. I tell her just that.

"Very sexy."

"Really?"

I shrug a shoulder. "Why would I lie?"

"Because our friends are here and you don't want me to change."

"I promise, you look great, Froggie."

I swing open the front door, and it seems everyone is here. Everyone except…"Where's Bex?"

"She got stuck on a call with the league, so she's going to try and be here later."

"We'll miss her," Alice says. "She was fun in Vegas."

"We were a little intoxicated then." Cash laughs.

"Hey, it's not our fault we won the Stanley Cup." Troy laughs, as everyone funnels in.

"It's easy to get shit-faced when we're celebrating," I say.

"Hopefully we'll be bringing more home soon," Cash says.

"Not if Noah has anything to say about it," Piper retorts.

I snort laugh. "Having played for the Knights? That's wishful thinking."

"Hey, you never know," Piper says. "They could bring one home in a few years."

"Okay, who are you cheering for?" Cash asks. "Your brother or boyfriend?"

"I'd like to be cheering for my fiancé, but…" She pins him with a fierce stare, wiggling her fingers at him.

"Yeah, yeah. I know."

"Still no ring," she replies in a singsong as she heads into the kitchen with the rest of the women.

"You haven't done it yet?" I whisper to Cash.

"No, he's waiting for his day with the Cup," Nick says. "Isn't that next week?"

He nods, shaking his head. "But Piper is dropping every kind of hint shy of dropping a jewelry store on my head."

"Do you at least have the ring?" Troy asks as we head to the wet bar to make drinks.

He nods. "It's in my locker at the rink."

"Seriously?" Nick asks.

"Knowing Piper, she'd go snooping and I don't want her to ruin the surprise."

I smile, clapping him on the shoulder. "I love it, man. She definitely gives you a run for your money."

"Yeah, yeah. I need a drink if we're going to continue discussing this," Cash says. "Why can't we discuss Nicky's love life?"

"Hey. I do not want to be discussing this," he scoffs. "And technically, she's your boss so maybe let's not talk about her?"

I point a finger at him. "He does have a point."

"It's not like she's going to use anything against you outside of the rink," Nick says. "Unless you do something stupid."

"Liable with this guy." Cash smacks me in the bicep.

"Asshole. I make great decisions."

"Like getting married when you're drunk in Vegas?" Troy asks.

"That was a great decision," I clarify.

The doorbell rings again, and Alice walks over to grab it.

"Leon. Jacob. I'm so glad you could make it." She hugs both of them.

"Sorry we're late," Jacob bemoans. "Someone had to change his outfit a few times."

I walk over to where they're standing and take the flowers from Leon's hands. "These look great."

"And *you* look great," Alice says. "And the flowers."

"Thank you." Leon pecks her on the cheek. "We mostly left on time, but you know traffic out here."

"Just in time. Let's get you a drink and then we can eat."

They follow Alice into the kitchen as Cash calls attention to him.

"I think a toast is in order before dinner," Cash says. Everyone holds up their drinks as he continues. "It's been great having you on the team, Paddy, and I'm glad we can all get together before the season officially starts next week to celebrate your wedding."

Grabbing Alice's hand, I pull her close. "I love being a part of this team, and I appreciate you guys being so welcoming to both of us."

"It's been great," Alice agrees. "It's nice having girlfriends."

"Excuse me," Leon interjects. "What am I?"

"You're still one of my closest friends here. That's not changing," she answers.

"Good." He blows her a kiss.

"You're more than welcome to hang out with all of the girls too, Leon," Piper says.

"I like you," Leon tells her.

Alice squeezes me close, and I know how much it means to her to have these people in her life. I know Leon and I joked about her not having much work-life balance, but she loves Enchanted Petals, and it's hard to pull her away from it.

For them to readily accept her as part of the group? I know she loves it.

"Okay, time to eat," I say.

"Thank God. I'm starving." Cash goes into the kitchen and grabs a plate to help himself to barbecue.

"What he means to say is thanks." Piper shakes her head. "I can't take him anywhere."

"Hey, they like me. It's okay."

"So you think," Troy calls back.

Cash flips him the bird.

"If it helps, you're definitely my husband's favorite player," Jacob says, following them into the kitchen.

"It's nice to see they're all getting along," I whisper to Alice.

She smiles up at me. "Do you think they're all going to gang up on us at some point?"

I look at everyone that's gathered at our house. "Oh, absolutely."

"Are you two going to eat or just stare at us all night?" Cash asks.

"We are pretty people." Leon chuckles next to him.

"Damn straight." Cash laughs.

"Yup," Alice says. "Totally going to gang up on us at some point."

Leaving my side, she walks over to grab her own dinner.

When I got traded to the Black Diamonds, the one thing I was most excited for was playing for a winning team. That, and being in the same city as Alice. I never thought that I'd become so close with the guys.

It's nice having a group of people able to spend so much time together and know that we're all having the same experience. Alice gets to have women who will support her and be there for her while I'm gone. It's not like she doesn't have work and Leon, but I know she's always prioritized work.

She loves it. It's part of the reason we're doing what we're doing.

"Did you guys hear what happened with Toronto's forward?" Nick asks as I head into the kitchen.

"No. What?" I ask, scooping a pile of mac and cheese onto my plate.

"He got cut because apparently the team found out he was sleeping around while on road trips and using the hotel rooms the team paid for to throw big parties to bring women in."

And there's the other reason we're doing what we're doing. The league wants to clean up their image because of guys like him.

"He deserves it," Piper says. "I don't know how people like him or Duncan are still in the league."

"Easy, Princess." Cash kisses her head.

"Ugh. Sorry. I hate people like that who treat women like objects to be used and tossed aside."

"It's why the league is cracking down," Troy says.

Don't I know it. Stupid, drunken behavior in Vegas? Not the best optics for the league.

Alice isn't looking at me as she walks over to the table and takes a seat next to Leon. Knowing her, her face would give her away.

Things quiet down as everyone piles into chairs around the dining room table and digs into their food.

"I'm not the biggest hockey fan," Jacob says, breaking the silence.

Cash's fork clatters to his plate. "Seriously?"

Leon shakes his head. "Don't look at me. I've tried."

"Since we're with half the Black Diamonds team—"

"More like a quarter," Nick interjects.

"Maybe one of you could convince me to watch it. You know, get your jersey and all that."

"Wow." Leon looks at him, incredulously. "I've tried getting you to watch the game with me for years, and all it takes is bringing a few players around?"

"Sorry." He shrugs.

"Way to go, Alice. You've been holding out on me," Leon says.

"Hey!" she exclaims. "I've brought Declan around plenty."

"How is this my fault?" I ask, wiping my mouth and setting it down on my empty plate.

"You were supposed to convince my husband to like hockey." Leon says this like it's the most obvious thing in the world.

"Declan shouldn't be the favorite then," Cash says. "I should be the favorite because I'm the best player."

"Hey!"

Troy and Nick scoff at the same time.

"I like the confidence," Jacob says. "Maybe if you play well in the first game, I'll buy your jersey."

"Seriously, I feel like chopped liver over here," I whine.

"Aww." Alice kisses my cheek. "You're still my favorite player."

"See? You're covered," Leon states. "I always go for goalies."

A furious blush creeps up over Nick's cheeks. He hates being the center of attention.

"He's my favorite on the days my husband is annoying me." Angie laughs.

"Ouch. Way to make a guy feel unloved," Troy fires back.

"And on the days you're really annoying me, you're number three."

"Number three? Who's two?" Alice asks.

"Lydia, his sister. She plays for Boston," Angie explains.

Alice smiles back. "I guess I'll have to start watching her play."

"You should. The PWHL is great. They're supposed to be expanding next season, which I think is exciting," Angie says.

"Who knows, maybe Denver will end up with a team and she'll come out here," Troy says.

"Okay, let's start with one team." Jacob laughs. "I need to get started with the men's team before I start women's."

"Fair," Alice says. "Maybe you can come to a game with me sometime."

"Do I get an invite?" Leon says. "I actually like the team."

"Sure—"

"Only if you stop bugging me about my work-life balance," Alice interrupts.

He rolls his eyes before blowing her a kiss. "Fine. Only because I love you and I'm glad you found a husband."

"That makes two of us," I agree, tipping my glass in his direction.

I don't care if it was a drunken decision in Vegas. Getting to call Alice my wife?

I'll soak up every minute of that I can.

Chapter Twenty

DECLAN

"Would you stop pacing? You're going to put a dent in the carpet."

"I can't help it. I want it to be here."

Alice laughs at me, walking from the kitchen to give me a cup of coffee. "You still have ten minutes before they're supposed to come."

"You know…"

"Don't get any ideas," Alice says, dropping down onto the couch and kicking her feet up.

Lifting them, I sit next to her and pull them into my lap. "Damn. It definitely would have taken my mind off things."

Alice sips her coffee, already looking as beautiful as ever. Given that today is my day with the Cup, we were both up before the sun rose. With the season starting in just a few weeks, I've had this day in my mind for weeks.

Hell, I've been dreaming of this since I was a kid. What kid doesn't grown up imagining winning the Stanley Cup and getting to have their day with it?

A knock sounds from the front door.

"Thank God." Leaping over the back of the couch, I swing open the front door.

There it is. In all its glory.

"Mr. Paddack. Hi, I'm John Bellville."

I shake the man's hand. He's dressed in a pressed black suit with a black tie and white gloves.

"Hi."

Opening the door wider, I beckon him inside. Alice's eyes track the trophy as it's brought into the living room and set on the coffee table.

"You're aware of the rules?" he asks.

"Yes."

We were all given a lecture from Coach Barney not to do anything to embarrass ourselves—or the team—on our day. Notices also landed in our lockers on clean-out day on how our behavior directly reflects on the team.

It's why I have an easy day planned.

"Good. Then we'll have a good day together."

"You're here all day?" Alice asks.

"Sorry. Alice, John. John, Alice." I introduce them, but I don't take my eyes off the gleaming silver trophy that fills the living room.

"Nice to meet you."

"You too, ma'am. I'll be around, but as long as you don't do anything to damage the Cup, you won't notice me."

"I'll try and keep him in line."

"Hey." I glance at her, before looking back at the Cup. "Holy shit."

"What?" Alice asks, coming to stand next to me.

"There's my name."

I run my finger over it, tracing the etchings.

Declan Paddack.

"Wow."

Alice leans down next to me, both of us staring at my name. Right there. Forever in the history of the game.

She presses a kiss to my cheek. "I'm so proud of you."

"I never thought this would happen."

Going from the worst team in the league to the best was something I only dreamed of happening. Getting to spend the day with the Stanley Cup? It was a far-off fantasy.

Now? Now it's sitting in my living room.

"Ready to spend your day with the Cup?"

GETTING into the suite at the Denver Miners game, our professional baseball team, took a lot longer than I thought. Carrying the Cup through the ballpark was like a giant beacon to have everyone stop and take a picture with it.

After drinking a mostly Champagne breakfast out of the Cup, Alice and I took it to the shop so she could show Leon and Jacob. They loved it. From there, we decided to come to a baseball game.

I mean, what fans don't want to see the Stanley Cup?

"Mr. Paddack. Congratulations on winning." The suite attendant bustles up to us as we come inside.

"Thank you." I set the Cup at my feet and shake his hand.

"We have seats saved up front for you. Help yourself to whatever you'd like, and if you need anything, let us know."

"We appreciate it," Alice tells him. "Thank you."

Eyes follow us as we take the first row. Fans below us, ready for the game, turn and eye the Cup as we drop down into the leather seats.

"They are really rolling out the red carpet for you," Alice says.

"I think it's for the Cup," I say.

"Either way, I'm glad you get to celebrate today. You deserve it."

I beam at her. The best part of today is that she's by my side. I wouldn't want anyone else with me. Even though we've been posting pictures of our day on social media to keep up appearances, it's not a chore.

Getting to spend the day with my wife *and* my best friend?

What else could I want?

"You know," Alice starts, "I really don't know much about baseball."

"It's okay. We're here to have fun."

"I mean, hockey is about all I can stand."

"All you can stand?" I quirk a brow at her.

"It's stressful watching you play. I can't add in any more sports."

Laughter bubbles out of me. "Good to know. You want anything to drink?"

"I'll take a beer."

"You got it."

People clap me on the back and offer their congratulations as I grab us drinks and plates of snacks. The national anthem rings out, signaling the start of the game is close.

By the time I get back to our seats, Alice is standing and cheering as the game starts. In a Black Diamonds hat, her long blonde hair flows down her back, while she wears a white T-shirt with dark jean shorts. She is the most beautiful person I've ever seen in my life.

I've always known Alice is beautiful. Before anything could happen, we became best friends. I never wanted to jeopardize that.

Even the thought now of this thing ending makes my heart crack in my chest. I want Alice. *Only* Alice. But that's something I'm going to have to broach later. She only just took this thing to the next level. I don't want to make her overthink things.

"Took you long enough," she says, as I hand her one of the beers.

"Sorry."

"You're okay. We're up."

As if on cue, the crack of a bat rings out as one of the Miners' players takes off to first base. He makes it before the ball hits the glove of the baseman. I guess it was a fast three up and down for the other team.

I clap along with everyone else as the next hitter lines up.

"Did you ever think about playing another sport?" Alice asks.

I shake my head. "Nope. You know I was in skates practically as soon as I could walk."

"But it never crossed your mind?"

"All I ever wanted to play was hockey."

"It's a good thing you're good at it."

"Would you come to my baseball games if I played for the Miners?"

"Hell, yeah. You know I would. It's a good thing you can't come watch me work."

"Is that supposed to be a challenge?" I ask. "Because if I could, I'd come watch you make bouquets every day."

"Stop it." She pushes me away. "You'd be so bored."

"Getting to be with you, Froggie? It's never boring."

She sips on her drink, that all too familiar blush creeping up her cheeks. I love how easily she shows what she's feeling.

It's something she's always done.

The game goes on, the Miners scoring two runs in their half of the inning before Seattle is back up to bat. Before I know it, the kiss cam starts up. It flashes across couples around the field before it locks on to me and Alice.

"Oh my God!" Alice cries out, covering her face with her hands in embarrassment.

"You want me to kiss you?" I drop an arm around her shoulders.

"You have to. Otherwise, everyone is going to boo at us."

An idea comes to me. I lean in, Alice with her hands shielding our faces from the camera. At the very last minute, I dodge to the other side and kiss the trophy.

"Are you serious?" Alice shrieks next to me. "You kissed the Cup and not me?"

Cheers ring out around the ballpark, mixed with boos.

Laughter bursts out of me. "Hey, I only get to have the Cup for one day. *One*, Froggie. You can't blame a guy."

The camera pans back to us and this time, when I go to kiss Alice, she throws a hand up. My lips meet her palm as she sips from her beer.

"Ouch."

If possible, the cheers get even louder, the crowd enjoying my embarrassment.

"You deserve it."

"You know all of my *real* kisses are for you, Froggie."

Pulling her close, I seal my lips over hers. This one is for no one but us.

When I pull away, she follows, wanting more.

"Mmm," she whispers.

Her eyes are closed, face pink from the sun beating down on us.

"Does that make up for it?" I ask, pecking her once

again before turning my attention to the game that's resumed play.

"No."

"Really?" I grab her drink and sip from it. "Why not?"

"Because now I want more and that definitely won't be happening."

"You mean you don't want a quickie in the bathroom?" I waggle my brows at her.

"Stop it. That won't be happening. *Ever.*"

"Never say never, Froggie."

The rest of the afternoon goes by in haze of drinks, kissing Alice whenever I can, and people wanting to take pictures with the Cup as we make our way out of the ballpark.

"I don't think I've ever been more peopled out in my life," I say, collapsing on the couch.

"Really? You?"

Alice leans over the couch, hair curtaining around us.

"Everyone has their limits."

"Well, since we still have a few hours with the Cup, can we do one more thing?"

"Whatever you want, Froggie."

"Close your eyes."

The sounds of cabinets opening and closing bang around in my head. A happy buzz floats through my veins.

Today was the perfect day. Could I have done something bigger and better? Maybe. But I don't care. Getting to spend it with my favorite person was all I needed.

"Okay. Open your eyes."

Alice is holding the Cup, albeit awkwardly since it's so big. Fresh blooms sit in the bowl of it. Flowers I recognize well.

"It's my flower."

"I know it's cheesy—"

"It's not." I stop her, grabbing the Cup from her and resting it between us before standing.

Her blue eyes are soft, full of happiness. "Everyone has been celebrating you today everywhere we go, and I don't really know what I can do to show you how proud of you I am, so I figured this would be something."

"You already gave me my jersey." The very one that's hanging in the basement. "You don't have to give me anything, Froggie. Getting to spend the day with you was better than anything I ever could have imagined."

"Are you sure it wasn't the Cup?" She smiles.

Pushing my fingers through her hair, I drop my forehead to hers. "Maybe a little. But you made it better."

"Good."

I pull out my phone. "Now let's commemorate this moment."

"Are you going to post this?" she whispers against my lips.

I shake my head. "No. This one is just for us."

Her hands link behind my neck, the Cup between us. "Care to do something else just for us?"

"That's the best idea you've had all day." I smile. "I want to do whatever *my wife* wants to do."

Chapter Twenty-One

"I want to do whatever *my wife* wants to do."

Goose bumps break out all over my skin at Declan's words. I don't know if I'll ever get used to hearing him call me his wife.

"Shouldn't today be all about you?" I ask, straddling his lap.

He shakes his head. "Right now, it gets to be about you and what you want to do."

"Hmm." I tap a finger to my chin. "Whatever I want to do?"

His cock hardens between my thighs and I rock over him when an idea comes to mind.

"Whatever you fucking want." Declan presses warm kisses up and down my neck. I dig my fingers into his shoulders, heat and lust swirling in my veins.

"But first…"

Brushing my lips against his forehead, I head into the bedroom to grab a few things and come back out to find him in the kitchen. Declan grabs the cork of the bourbon bottle and rips it off before taking a swig.

"What's that for?" He nods to the lube in my hand.

"I was thinking that we could do a little ass play tonight."

Lust settles in his eyes. "Are you serious?"

I nod. "Yes. I liked it when you played with it, so why not see what it feels like with more?"

"Fuck."

Declan sets the bottle on the counter and hoists me up onto the counter, stepping between my legs.

He makes quick work of my shirt and bra before lavishing my breasts with attention. Each suck and nibble on my hard nipples has me arching into his touch.

With Declan, I'm wanton. I need more. Crave more.

He knows how to please me with one look.

"Declan, please."

"Please what?"

"More."

"What do you want?"

"I'm aching. I need you here." Grabbing his hand, I move it to the button of my jean shorts. "I want your mouth on me."

"Whatever you want. It's all about you tonight, Alice."

Declan undoes the button and zipper with fast fingers before he tugs them off and drops them at his feet.

I'm completely naked and bare to him. He scoots me to the edge of the counter, opening my legs up to him. His eyes rake over me. Every gaze sets my skin on fire.

"Are you going to stare at me all night, or are you going to make me come?"

He grins at me, dropping down so his face hovers over my pussy. "You are so impatient."

His eyes stay locked on mine as he swipes his tongue through my wet folds.

"Yes!"

It's immediate relief as he moves his ministrations to my clit and circles his tongue over the tight bundle of nerves.

Declan keeps his focus on me as he eats me out. Each delicious lick and suck amps up my desire for the man and what we're going to do.

It's hard to keep focus on him as he devours me. My heels dig into his back, urging him on. When he dips a finger inside and drags it back to the tight pucker of my ass, it's all I can do not to explode.

"I can't wait to feel what it's like to fuck your ass," he says.

He pushes his finger inside and it feels incredible. Anything this man does to me is pure bliss.

"Then hurry up and make me come so you can do it."

I feel rather than see his smile as he picks up the pace. With the tip of his finger in my ass and his tongue licking inside me, I detonate.

"Declan!" My shouts echo in the kitchen as I come and come.

It feels endless, but Declan stays between my thighs, licking up every last drop.

I fall back onto my elbows, completely blissed out.

"Fuck, Alice." Declan leans over me, chin wet with my release. "You look so damn sexy like this. All spread out for me."

"You make me feel so damn good, Dec," I huff out, my breathing starting to return to normal.

"You ready for more?" he asks.

I nod. "Give it to me."

Standing back, Declan sheds his clothes, his dick springing out of his briefs and smacking him in the stomach. He grabs the bottle of lube and pours a generous amount in his palm before giving himself a long, slow stroke.

"Think you can stand?"

I hop off the counter with his assistance before he's kissing me.

Greedy. Hungry. Full of passion.

I can't get enough of this man's mouth on me.

"Turn around."

I do as he says, and he pulls my hips back against him. He slips a wet finger through my crack before playing with my rim.

"Mmm."

His weight settles over me as he pushes the tip inside.

"I love getting to play with you like this."

Wiggling back against him, I take more of him in. I'm full in a way I've never experienced but knowing I'll get more urges me.

"More, Dec. More."

"I don't want to hurt you," he whispers.

"You won't."

He pushes two fingers inside, scissoring them to open me. I throw my head back in delight.

As he continues to work me over, his lips trail up and down my shoulder. His touch is overwhelming in the best way. After one orgasm, I could easily come like this again.

"You ready?" Declan whispers.

"Yes."

"Then hands on the counter."

The snick of the lube bottle opening splits the quiet air as he drizzles more down my crack before lining the blunt head of his cock up. It's an odd sensation as he pushes inside, but he takes his time.

Going slow, inch by slow inch to let me stretch to his size.

"Declan. Oh my God."

His fingers dig into my hips, holding on tighter. "Fuck, Alice. The way your ass is squeezing my dick? Fuck."

"It's so good," I answer, knowing we're both feeling the same thing.

I've never done this before—had someone in my ass. Only Declan. It feels so good as he starts to move. Reaching between us, I strum my clit.

"You need more?" he whispers against my neck.

"Faster."

"Like I said, whatever you want tonight."

He picks up the pace, moving in and out as he slides one free hand around to play with my nipples.

It's sensory overload. Every single nerve ending is on fire. Sweat clings to my brow as I get closer and closer to coming again.

"Alice," Declan growls, biting at the tender skin of my neck. "Fuck. I need to come."

"Then do it."

"Not before you."

He pulls back, grabbing my hips and slamming into me.

"Gah!"

The only sound now is skin against skin as he pounds into me.

"Holy fuck."

Declan's orgasm slams into him, taking me right over the edge with him.

And holy shit. It's so damn good that I drop to my chest on the counter as he stills inside me, both of us riding our highs.

The granite cools my overheated skin as I try to catch my breath.

Declan pulls out of me, and the rush of the sink water

fills my ears before he comes back to clean me up. His touch is so gentle, it pulls a smile to my face.

"I like this side of you, Alice."

Declan scoops me into his arms and carries my limp body into the living room. The two of us lie on the couch together as Declan drags a blanket over our naked selves.

"Oh, yeah?"

He combs his fingers through my hair. "Yeah. You don't have a care in the world and just give yourself over to me. I love it."

"You make it easy to do." I sigh against his chest.

"Talk about the best ending to this day."

"It's been pretty great."

"We should probably go to bed," he says.

I burrow in closer, not wanting to move. "Probably."

"I should probably also give the Cup back."

The two of us drift off just like this.

The perfect ending to the perfect day.

Just how I want all of my days to be.

With Declan.

Chapter Twenty-Two

ALICE

"You know, this was the perfect way to spend the afternoon," I say.

Walking hand in hand with Declan, we stroll through the aquarium. The sounds of happy children echo around us.

It might not be the most exciting of dates, but it'll be the last one we can squeeze in before the regular season starts next week.

"I'm glad Leon let you off."

"You know him—he's all about me and that work-life balance." I smile at him.

"I really enjoy this new equilibrium you're trying to employ." Declan presses a kiss to my temple as we walk into the shark exhibit.

"Hey. Someone has to work around here. Besides, I don't think the life of a professional athlete is the definition of balance."

Declan drapes an arm around my shoulder as we head into the dark, cavernous room.

"Hey, if we're going to defend our title, I might be a

little MIA." He raps his knuckle on the closest hard surface.

"I for one hope that happens."

"Hey! Knock on wood." Declan looks at me like I've committed a grave error because I didn't somehow acknowledge that it might jinx them.

"Athletes and your superstitions."

"See if I take you out on my Cup day again."

"To be stood up on the kiss cam? I'll pass." I laugh.

I shake my head as I pull him toward the thick glass. Sharks lazily swim by. Fish scurry past as seaweed moves with the current.

It's peaceful, standing here in the dark and watching them go about their days. Not a care in the world.

"Hey." Declan wraps his arms around my waist and pulls me back against him, dropping his chin on my shoulder. "You did give me the hand, Froggie."

"Only after you kissed the Cup instead."

"Sue me. You know I only had a day with it. I have a whole year with you."

I swallow down the emotions that threaten to bubble up at the thought of being done with Declan in a year.

It seems the two of us have only just gotten started, but I don't want to lose him. I mean, he's my best friend. We'll always be best friends. But this new place the two of us are in? I really like it.

He's been my best friend since I puked all over his tennis shoes and he took care of me, not once trying to sleep with me. Whenever anyone questioned our friendship, we always brushed it off. I mean, how could you fall in love with someone when they puke all over you?

But now? Now things feel different. The more we act like a couple, the more it feels like we *are* a couple.

Based on Declan's comment, he doesn't seem to mind the end date this thing between us has.

Oohs and aahs bring me out of my thoughts. Faces are pressed up against the glass as kids try to follow the sharks.

"Would you want to be a shark?" I ask, needing to steer myself back to a better headspace.

"I mean, I'd be at the top of the food chain, so why not?"

"Kind of like the Black Diamonds?"

"Aren't you funny?" He tickles my side.

"It's why you love me so much."

"Yeah, yeah."

I grab his hand and head toward the tunnel connecting the exhibits. Fish move all around us. It's like we're a part of their world like this, as they're coming at us from all sides.

"I wish the season weren't starting," I confess.

"Why's that?" Declan asks, looking down at me.

"I know it's going to get busy for you, but I like that we get to do things like this together."

"Just because the season is starting, Froggie, doesn't mean we can't do this."

"With what free time?"

"Fair, but it's not like I won't make time for you," he says, leading us out of the tunnel and toward the dolphin exhibit.

The water in here is still before a dolphin zooms past. Another one is quick to follow, racing in circles in their tank.

"Ooh, look!" I point to a scuba diver floating halfway down. "I would love to try that someday."

"Really? You would?" he asks.

"Yes. It's something I've always wanted to learn."

"How did I not know this?"

"You don't know *everything* about me, Dec."

"Alice, please. I've known you for almost a decade. I know more about you than I know about myself."

"Not everything, apparently."

"Umm, Alice? What are those two doing?"

Declan's hand points to the other side of the exhibit, and—

"Oh my God!" I cover my mouth, trying not to laugh.

"Are they really going at it?" I can hear the amusement in his voice.

"I mean, they did say when we got here that we'd get an immersive experience."

"Mommy, what are those two doing?" a nearby child asks.

"Come on, dear. Let's go pet the stingrays."

The mom grabs her kid's hand and tugs them away.

"Someone isn't up for a biology lesson," Declan whispers. "It's all a part of the circle of life. Maybe I should break it to the kid."

I turn, burying my laughter in his chest. Other kids are still pointing at the two dolphins in the corner.

"I think you might traumatize the mother if you did that."

She's still trying to get her kid to leave, but they're still eyeing the dolphins like they're the coolest mammals around.

"If we brought our kids here and they saw that, we would definitely be telling them what's happening," Declan says with no hint of argument in his tone.

"Are you serious? You cannot tell our kids about dolphins having sex."

"What? It's a perfectly natural part of life."

"And what happens when that leads to other questions about sex?" I quirk a brow at him.

"Okay, now you're getting into a weird territory, Froggie."

"You just said it's a natural part of life."

"Fine. I see your point."

"Good. I don't want little Declans running around school telling all their friends how dolphins are made."

"We would definitely get a call from their teacher."

I smile at him as we walk away, leaving the dolphins to themselves.

"Something I'd let you deal with, Dec."

"Maybe I could bribe them with Black Diamonds tickets."

"Assuming you're still with the team."

"What's that supposed to mean?" he asks, affronted. "Don't even joke about that."

"If we're talking about taking our hypothetical children to the aquarium, they have to be at least seven or eight, especially if we're getting calls from the teacher about how they're misbehaving in class."

"Okay, fair."

"And as much as I love you, Declan, professional athletes retire much earlier than the average person."

"Again, seriously? You're killing me, Froggie."

The room in front of us opens to a small, fenced-off pool of water. Kids are crowded around the plastic barriers. Through the glass, we can see stingrays swimming in the touch tank.

"I take it we won't bring our kids to the aquarium then?"

"Maybe not even the zoo."

"Then we better pet the rays before you ban us from coming." I wink at him and dart over to an opening between people. After reading the sign on how to do this, I brush two fingers along the back of a small stingray as it swims by.

"How does it feel?" Declan asks.

I turn to face him, and he snaps a picture of me.

I smile at him. "Weird."

"This whole day is weird." He laughs. "I'm learning new things about you, plus there's the mating dolphins."

"Aww. Is your poor mind blown?" I kiss his cheek, pulling him close so he can touch the stingray too.

"Maybe."

Declan mirrors what I'm doing as he pets the ray that comes toward him. I rest my chin on his shoulder as I watch him.

His happiness is infectious. This is what I've always loved about him. He finds so much joy in everything he does.

He's been like this ever since I met him.

"Okay, I kind of want a pet stingray now," he says, sticking his hand under the sanitizer and rubbing it around.

I do the same.

"I am not letting you get a pet stingray when you won't be home to take care of it."

"That's the only reason?" He quirks a brow at me.

"That and I don't want to take care of it."

"You're no fun."

Spying the small café on the other side of the room, I nod my head in that direction. "Then how about we get some snow cones instead. Will that help soften the blow?"

"Only if I can pay."

"Fine."

Standing in line, I notice the eyes that follow Declan. It's easy to spot him wherever we go. People now easily recognize him as one of the Black Diamonds. I love that he's getting the attention he deserves. A few people ask to take photos with him as I order us two snow cones.

"That'll be thirty dollars," the man behind the counter says.

"I'm sorry, what?" Declan pops up, confusion written on his face.

"Two snow cones with three flavors each is thirty dollars," he repeats.

"Thirty dollars?" Declan taps his credit card on the machine. "That's insanity."

"Thank you." I press up onto my toes to give his cheek a kiss.

Grabbing the two holders, I follow Declan to a small table for two set in the corner.

"You better enjoy every damn ounce of that," he says, grabbing his cone. "I mean, thirty dollars? Holy shit."

"Technically it's only fifteen."

"Fine. Enjoy every bite of your *fifteen*-dollar snow cone."

I stab the paper straw into it and suck out a bite. Sugary goodness bursts on my tongue. "You know I will."

"Damn, this is good."

"Fifteen dollars' worth?" I ask.

"Yeah, yeah."

I slurp up more of my treat as Declan watches me from across the metal table.

"What?"

"Do you really not know what you're doing?"

He shifts around, an almost pained expression flashing across his face.

I smile back at him. "Can I not enjoy my fifteen-dollar snow cone?"

"Not when you're driving me crazy with it."

A knowing look fills his blue eyes. Damn. Seeing him like this drives me equally as wild.

"You want to cut this afternoon short?"

"No, because I want to pet the stingray one more time."

"And then you want to cut it short?"

"I wouldn't be opposed. Maybe give you a real lesson on how babies are made."

I snort before taking a bite of my blood orange, cherry, and pineapple snow cone. "Mmm. I like that idea."

"Okay, you're teasing me."

"You're the one that started it."

The rest of the afternoon goes by in a blur of laughs, fish, petting stingrays, and another visit to the shark tank.

It's not until the ride home—with Declan's hand splayed across my thigh—that the afternoon really starts to sink in and the discussions that we had. This thing has an end date, but here we were discussing our children.

Hypothetical children.

Right now, I have no idea what the future holds. My biggest priority—my *only* priority—is getting Enchanted Petals. After that, I can figure the rest out.

But being with Declan? Talking about our kids?

It's not our future.

No matter how badly I may want it.

Chapter Twenty-Three

DECLAN

"Crowd is fired up today," Cash says, shooting a puck my direction before I fire it into the goal during warm-ups.

Looking around, I'm surprised to see that most of the fans are here earlier than normal. That new-season excitement is a living breathing thing in the arena.

Even more so because we're unveiling our championship banner.

And I get to do it with my wife in the crowd.

"I've never done anything like this."

"You mean play hockey?" Troy jests.

I do my best to flip him off in my gloves.

"I mean get to be part of a championship ceremony like this."

"Couldn't have done it without you, man," Cash says.

"I think that might be the nicest thing you've ever said to me."

"Yeah, yeah. Don't get used to it."

Cash goes back to firing the puck at the goal as I do a few more laps around the ice to get my legs warmed up.

People are pounding the glass as we all skate around the rink.

God, I love this feeling.

The entire season is before us. Every team is on the same playing field. No wins and no losses. Even though we get to celebrate our championship from last year, as soon as that banner is hung, all bets are off.

As we're called back to the locker room, I take one last look around the arena, now almost packed.

Fuck. I really can't wait for this game to get started.

I know where the family suite is and I know that Alice is here tonight.

I've always loved that she's come to my games. Even before we got married, she would come to my games. She was there at every college game, and whenever she could come to Nashville, she'd be there.

I like that she'll be here more often.

Hell, to almost every game if she can.

When I get back to the locker room, I can't sit still. Throwing my stick and gloves into my cubby, I pace around the Black Diamonds logo that rests in the middle of the carpet.

"You good?" Nick asks.

"Ready for the game to start."

"Might as well sit down. We still have thirty minutes before it starts."

"Right."

I plop down next to him, blowing out a breath.

My legs bounce as I do my best to calm my excited nerves as we tick closer and closer to the puck drop.

Before I know it, Coach Barney is walking into the locker room in his always pristine suit.

"Alright, gentlemen. I know we're all excited to get out

there and see our newest banner in the rafters, but there's a lot more than just celebrating tonight. Tonight, we start a new season. Fresh slate. I know the pressure that the outside noise can put on a team. But I want you to shut that out. I want each and every man in here to focus on your game. To play together as a *team*. That's what I want. It's a long season, and I want to go out there and start it off on the right foot. Let everyone talk. I know what our team can do. Now go out there and show me what you're made of."

"Hell, yeah!" Cash shouts. He corrals the team to the middle of the locker room. "Let's go out there and give our fans a show tonight! Black Diamonds on three. One, two…"

"Black Diamonds!" everyone yells.

Fuck. Yes.

I follow the other players out of the locker room as Troy—our captain—claps each of us on the helmet as we go.

When the team is announced, the crowd noise from earlier is nothing compared to now. It's fucking electric. It's a wave of blue in the stands as everyone sports the team colors. The lights are low as a video from last year's season starts. It's hard not to get pumped up when they're showing our highlights.

By the time they get to the part with the team lifting the Cup, the arena could break sound records with the noise pulsing inside.

The lights come up and the banner for last year's Stanley Cup is unveiled. Damn. I see these banners everywhere we play. It's nothing new.

But this is the first time I've been a part of one. To have contributed to the team winning it. And fuck, it feels amazing.

After the anthem is sung, Coach Barney calls us all back to the bench before the puck drop.

"Alright, gentlemen. I know it's cool to see that, but we need to put that behind us. Focus on our game. Focus on Anaheim. They are a good team, but I want to show them we're better."

I take my seat on the bench as the game starts. It gives me a chance to let my excitement settle and check out how the other team is playing.

No matter how much film we study, there's nothing like seeing our opponent in action.

It's clear Anaheim is good, but watching Cash and Troy work together? They are unstoppable as they move down the ice. Their stickhandling skills are unmatched.

Anaheim's goalie blocks a shot before their offense take it down the ice.

"Paddack. You're up."

Waiting until our guy is off the ice, I hop over the boards and start flying, skates crunching under me. Nick is ready for them and blocks the shot on goal with ease.

I can't marvel at his skill because I'm neck and neck with Cash as we head toward our zone.

Troy is there with the puck, firing it to me. Pulling my stick back, I shoot it at the goal. Anaheim's goalie easily blocks it, but I get the rebound. With Cash getting into position, I pass it to him and he is able to sneak it by the goalie, hitting the back of the net.

The horn sounds and the lamp lights up as the crowd erupts.

"Way to go, man!" I skate over and congratulate him.

"Great assist."

"Great job, guys!" Troy claps us each on the shoulder pads.

Fans are banging on the glass as we skate back to

center ice to resume the game. We're able to get the puck and put one more on the board before I'm heading back to the bench.

Damn, does it feel good to have an early lead. Still plenty of game to play, but skating with this group of guys? It feels fucking amazing.

"Great job out there, Paddack," Coach Barney tells me.

"Thanks, Coach."

I love how even-keeled he is. He never gets too excited about the wins or too down about the losses. I've only been playing for him since the middle of last season, but it's the kind of coach I've always wanted.

We keep Anaheim at bay during the second period, even getting another goal, but they start off the third period by scoring.

"Shit," I mutter, knocking my stick against the board.

"Paddack. Williams."

Cash and I take our positions on the ice.

"Let's do this, man." He bumps me in the chest with the butt of his stick.

"Fuck, yeah." I grin back at him.

I'm not going to let one goal get to me.

We win the face-off and Cash is on a tear. He charges straight toward their goalie, faking a shot before passing the puck back to me.

Pulling back, I aim and send the puck sailing over the glove and into the net.

"Yes!" I pump my arms in the air, jumping on Cash.

"Way to go, Paddy!"

It always feels good to get the first goal of the season under my belt. Takes the pressure off the need to score.

I skate back to the bench for the line change, and Troy is able to get another goal within a few minutes.

After that, it's smooth sailing.

We're able to hold them off until they get an easy shot late in the third. But it doesn't matter. By the time the final horn sounds, Colorado wins 5-2.

Everyone is jubilant as we skate back to the locker room, talking of celebrations and delayed workouts in the morning.

Me? All I can think about is getting to celebrate with my favorite person.

Hell, yeah.

Chapter Twenty-Four

ALICE

"I can't believe you found us a drive-in to come to tonight."

"Did you want to do something else tonight?"

"What? No." I laugh. "I didn't think they existed anymore."

Declan kisses the palm of my hand as he backs the truck into our designated spot. "This might be the last one."

"What's playing tonight?" I ask.

He shrugs a shoulder. "Beats me. I figured it'd be fun since we're getting ready to hit the road."

I sigh as the two of us get out to prepare the bed of the truck. Declan tosses pillows and blankets from the back seat and I spread them out before us.

"Do road trips get easier?" I ask, hopping down so the two of us can go grab some snacks.

"For who? Me or you?"

"Me."

The Black Diamonds were lucky to have a stretch of

home games to start the season, but now they'll be on the road for two weeks.

Declan smiles at me as we wait in the concession line. "Does that mean you're going to miss me?"

"I mean, kind of."

It's weird. I never missed Declan before now. But living with him these last few months, I've gotten so used to always having him around.

Even with long practice days and the preseason, he was gone while I was at work. We'd come home and talk about our days and have dinner together. We settled into a nice rhythm.

Not having him around is going to be a change.

"It's like you like me," he gloats.

"Yeah, yeah." I try to shove him away as we reach the counter, but he doesn't let me go.

"We'll take the nachos, pretzels, sour straws, and two waters." Declan looks down at me. "Anything else?"

"Is that all for you?" I ask.

"For both of us," he says.

"Add in popcorn and we're good."

Declan hands over cash, then drops a twenty in the tip jar as a box of food is pushed our way. He takes it and I grab the water bottles as we weave our way through the cars back to the truck.

Extending a hand, Declan helps me up.

Cars fill in the space around us as we dig in to all the snacks. As the sky turns to an inky velvet, the lights turn off and the movie starts.

The first of the double feature? An animated movie for kids that has the adults laughing almost immediately.

"I wish I had known you in high school," Declan says.

I tear off the end of a straw. "Oh, yeah? Why's that?"

"Maybe we would've started dating then and I could have taken you here on dates. Pretended to be really cool and try and kiss you."

"Would I have gotten your letterman jacket?"

"No one else I would have given it to."

He smacks a noisy kiss on my cheek.

"You know I was not cool in high school. Probably not very cool in college either."

"Well, I know one thing about you." Declan laughs.

"What's that?"

"You never could hold your liquor."

I snort laugh, trying not to choke over the sip of water I took.

"If I could, do you think we would have met?" I ask.

"I hope so. I mean, can you imagine if we hadn't?"

"I don't even want to think about that. I'd ruin your shoes ten times over if it meant we got to meet."

"Worth it, Froggie." Declan pulls me close. "There's nowhere else I'd rather be tonight than with you."

I snuggle in, leaning against him. A cool breeze blows through. The mountains reach up behind the movie screen toward the night sky.

Everything about this moment is perfect. Happiness burns bright inside my chest. With the smell of impending fall hanging in the air, it seems like more than just the seasons are changing.

Things with Declan have never been better.

When we decided to stick this out for a year, I thought we'd be living together, but separately. Keeping our lives as they were.

They've merged so effortlessly, that I don't know how I'll ever go back to not having him like this. Maybe we were always waiting around for each other and that drunken weekend in Vegas was just the catalyst to become more.

Declan is my person. Even before he became my husband, he was the one that I celebrated everything with. The wins, the losses, and everything in between.

It's easy to ignore the outside noise when I'm with him.

The guys in the league that are tarnishing the good names of other players? Easy.

Repeated emails and calls from my father wanting me to go work for him? No big deal.

Everything is right with Declan, and I want to hang on to this feeling for as long as possible.

"You're awfully quiet tonight, Froggie," Declan says.

I tilt my chin up, resting it on his chest. "You know you're not supposed to talk during movies, right?"

He taps me on the nose. "You know no one can hear us, right? And this movie is almost as old as we are."

"Fair. I want to enjoy our night together before you leave."

"I don't know if you know this, but there was something invented called the telephone. We can use it to talk to each other."

"I think I might have heard of it."

"Play your cards right tonight and I might just give you my number."

Swinging my leg over his lap, I link my fingers behind his neck. His hands move automatically, settling on my hips.

"*If* I play my cards right, hmm?"

I twirl my fingers through the soft locks of hair at the nape of his neck. The low lights scattered around the open field of the drive-in reflect back in his blue eyes. Ones that are filled with desire.

"I mean, I can't just give it to you," he states.

I ghost my lips over the shell of his ear. "Do you think if we make out I might be able to get it?"

The corner of his mouth cocks up in a grin. "Froggie, you can get anything you want."

"Then I can't wait to see what later will get me."

Chapter Twenty-Five

Tonight has been a lesson in patience.

Every single one of my fantasies of getting to do this with Alice back in high school came to life as we made out not only during the first movie, but the second too.

Whatever Alice does turns me on.

Anytime she is near me, I want to be close to her. I don't know when I fell head over heels for her, but I did. A complete goner.

Right now? Her hand is moving dangerously close to my hard cock. The one that has been painfully hard since we left the drive-in.

The only thing that matters is the house is finally in sight.

Thank fuck.

"Someone seems a little worked up."

She's leaning across the console now, moving closer to me.

"If it weren't for you, I'd be fine."

It takes all my willpower to drive the speed limit. No

point in getting into a wreck thirty seconds before we get home.

It's like the garage door is tormenting me as it slowly moves up. Not fast enough for my liking.

By the time I get the car parked, I reach over and pull Alice onto my lap. I roll my hips up, letting her feel exactly what she is doing to me.

"Do you need help taking care of this?"

"You know I do."

"Then what are you waiting for?"

Opening the door, I scoot out and lift Alice into my arms. Her legs wrap around my waist as she attacks my face and neck with kisses. I barely make it inside before I'm pressing her against the wall.

My mouth crashes against hers. Desperate to have her in a way I've never felt before. Her fingers hold me close as I find the buttons on her shirt and start to undo them.

Setting her on her feet, I shift my attention to her breasts. Hard peaks poke through the soft fabric of her bra. I tug one nipple between my teeth.

Whimpers and mewls hit my ears as I shift to the other one. I dip my fingers below the hem of her leggings and pull them down. A wet spot blooms on her underwear.

"How long have you been like this?" I ask, rubbing a finger against the fabric.

"About as long as you've been hard."

I take Alice in. I haven't done much besides kiss her and she already looks ravaged.

"You ready for more?" I ask.

"God yes, Dec." I grab her hand and lead her into the bedroom. "I want—"

"Not tonight," I interject. "Tonight, I choose."

"Then do it."

Cocking a smile at her, I help her out of her shirt before unhooking her bra and tossing it behind me.

"Do you know how much I love seeing you like this? What I do to you?"

My hands roam over her body, touching every inch of exposed skin. I peel her leggings off of her, leaving her naked in front of me. Her sweet scent draws me in. I nip and suck at her thighs. Lick her hip bones.

"More, Dec. More."

Scooping her into my arms, I move toward the bed and toss her into the center. She lands with a laugh. Blonde hair flows out around her head as she spreads her legs in welcome.

I strip out of my clothes and give myself a long, slow stroke to keep myself together.

"I'm going to miss you so much while I'm gone."

"Not as much as I'm going to miss you."

I smile down at her, pressing one knee into the mattress. "Then I guess I better make this good for you to tide you over until I'm back."

Alice reaches between her legs and pushes a finger into her pussy. "You better."

"Fuck. You look so damn sexy like this, but I think you need some help."

Grabbing her hand, I push it in and out, helping her get herself off. "Are you going to make me come?"

"Yes. You're going to get nice and wet for me so when I fuck you, you'll be ready."

"Yes," she hisses.

I suck on her clit as we both work together toward her release. I flick it and roll the tiny bundle of nerves around my tongue.

She's arching into my touch. I push her legs wider to

deepen my reach, moving my tongue lower to taste her wetness.

"Fucking delicious."

"I'm so close."

It only takes a few more swipes over her clit before she comes, coating my chin with her release.

"That's it."

She rocks into my touch as I carry her through her orgasm.

"So good, Declan."

Her body is limp beneath me as I sit up between her spread legs. I wipe my mouth.

"Turn over."

Alice obeys my command. God, her fucking ass is perfect. If I weren't so needy to bury my cock inside her pussy, I'd take her ass again.

Grabbing each of her legs, I push them up and open. Like this? Hell, she looks like…"my little Froggie."

Not wasting another second, I push inside her in one long, slow stroke.

"Declan. That feels amazing."

I cover her body with my own. I have to be close to her. Skin to skin contact. My moves are slow and deliberate. Her pussy is still pulsing around me, squeezing me as I keep driving inside.

I link hands with her, holding on tight. My balls are heavy, damn near close to coming. Being amped up all night has me on edge. My skin prickles as I feel her shifting beneath me.

"You close, Froggie?"

"Yes," she huffs out. "Oh God, yes."

Reaching between us, I find her clit again and roll it between my fingers.

That's all it takes. She's coming again.

"Yesss," I hiss. Pushing up on my hands, I increase my movements. I need to go with her. To come. To unleash inside of her.

Each squeeze and moan of hers eggs me on. It's not long before I'm coming inside her.

I throw my head back in relief, as the tension leaves my body. Pulling back, I groan as I watch some of my cum slip out of her.

Will I ever get used to this? I push my cum back inside as she moans in delight. I'm marking her as mine. *Only mine.*

And I never want to let her go.

I want to be with Alice.

For real.

I need to figure it out. No. I need to plan something for when I get back from the road trip. Sit her down and tell her how I feel. This isn't something one does over the phone.

Alice is special, and she deserves someone who will pull out all the stops for her. It might take some time to plan, but based on how happy she is? I hope she'll say yes.

Because Alice Burke being my wife? For real?

Nothing would make me happier.

Chapter Twenty-Six

ALICE

"You sure you want to do this?" Leon smacks a handful of papers down on the desk.

"Yes. If I'm going to run this place one day, I need to start doing this."

"I won't say no to the help."

"Anything I need to know?" I ask, flipping through the stack.

"Other than the fact that the computer is old and decides to crap out half the time? Save often."

He winks and is out the door.

"Thanks for nothing," I mutter.

Half the papers are invoices to be paid and the other half are orders mixed in to log into the system.

Shaking my head at Leon's organization, or lack thereof, I sort through everything to make my work easier.

The system isn't too difficult, but he wasn't wrong. It's slow and glitchy. Definitely something I can change when I take over.

Will it be in a year? Two years? I don't know, but once I get my trust, Enchanted Petals will be mine.

It's the only thing I've ever wanted to do. Spend my days surrounded by beautiful blooms and bringing people happiness through them.

Even the monotony of paperwork can't dampen my good mood at doing this. Stock ordered. Bills paid. Hours entered for our part-time employees. A few requests for events responded to.

Not bad for my first time doing this.

Flipping back to the events page, I'm already brainstorming ideas on what I can do. Weddings. Corporate events. The works.

It doesn't take much to get my creative juices flowing. A wedding with only white fabrics but they want a pop of color? I'm already imagining the palette of pink flowers I can use to complement what they're thinking.

This is one of my favorite things about working at Enchanted Petals.

"Someone is here to see you." Leon pops his head into the back office.

"There is?"

Sneaking a glance at my phone, I don't see any messages from Declan. It's not like it would be him. He should be at practice right now before their game in Vancouver tonight. It's the last night of a road trip and I cannot wait to see him. I've talked to him every chance I can get, and it still doesn't feel like enough.

I miss him more than I thought possible.

Then who in the world would be here?

Closing the laptop, I grab my apron, tying it around my waist before heading out front. The person I least expected to see is standing there, looking more out of place than ever.

"Mom?"

She spins on her low heels, pearl necklace resting against her chest.

"Alice. How are you?"

"I'm fine."

Walking around the counter, I give her a peck on the cheek. Standing next to her, the differences between the two of us are more apparent than ever.

Her dark hair is pinned perfectly in place, and her makeup is flawless. In a blouse with the collar popping out over her cardigan, her luxury handbag sits in the crook of her elbow.

Me? My blonde hair is in a messy bun and my jeans have new tears from the roses I trimmed last week.

"I wanted to come by and discuss the email your father sent you."

"Err, right."

Brown eyes are searching over the store. It's not the first time she's been here, but it's been a while. It's a judging eye. One that doesn't approve of what I'm doing with my life.

"By your reaction, I can see you received it."

"An entry-level analyst position." I nod. "Not exactly what I want to do."

Her nose turns up as she looks around the store again. "Alice, we have entertained this job long enough. The position at your father's firm is a prestigious one. You would be starting out making more than you make in a year here."

"Mom—"

"It's a good position, Alice. Stable. You never know what could happen with a place like this."

"You mean my livelihood."

"What about when you and Declan have a family? You can't spend all your time here playing with flowers."

"Is that really what you think I do? 'Play with flowers'?"

I put air quotes around her words.

"This isn't a real job, Alice," she snaps.

The store is quiet right now, with the only person here talking with Leon at the counter. His eyes keep flitting to mine. I only hope they can't hear this conversation.

"I'm not going to argue with you about this. I have things I need to do."

I don't know how many times I can have this conversation with them. I wish they would understand. Understand what I want to do with my life.

But they don't.

As I'm turning on my heel to head back to the office, she stops me.

"We expect you both at dinner next week."

"Me and Declan?"

"Yes." Her lips are drawn into a thin line.

It's her look of annoyance. No doubt because I dismissed her by ending the conversation early. Something I'm sure I'll hear about later.

"But—"

"Declan doesn't have a game. We already checked," she answers.

Shit. There goes my excuse.

"Will you send me the details?"

She nods, turning and leaving. The chimes ring out as the door closes behind her. Nerves are already settling in my stomach at the thought of having dinner with them.

"You okay?" Leon asks as I duck around the counter.

"Fine."

"You don't look fine."

"Just my mom doing my father's dirty work."

"Ahh." A knowing look washes over his face. "What position opened up?"

"Entry-level analyst."

He rolls his eyes. "Perfect if you love numbers."

"If only I did," I sigh, pushing open the office door to resume my work.

Maybe if I didn't like flowers so much, my parents might like me more. But it's the flowers I like. Working with numbers to make Enchanted Petals stay open? Those I can do.

Being elbow deep in floral creations every day is what I want to do. Not whiling away my time in an office with no windows.

I love the smell of flowers. The feel of the petals under my fingertips. Even the pinch of a thorn doesn't bother me.

Bold bouquets. Fresh centerpieces. Corsages for dances. Things that make people happy.

That's what I want to do. What I want to create.

I'm glad to have a husband who supports me. He's never tried to convince me I needed to do anything else and has always been my biggest cheerleader.

Having him in my corner means the world. Because I know with him by my side, Enchanted Petals will be mine when Leon decides to retire.

With the right person, it makes it easy to chase your dream.

Thank God for Declan.

Chapter Twenty-Seven

DECLAN

FROGGIE

Mom stopped by the store

DECLAN

Why?

She wanted to tell me about the job my dad
sent over

What job?

I hate being on the road

Some position at his company

Something I don't want

He kind of sucks

To put it mildly

She also invited us to dinner when you
get home

Ugh

Do we have to?

Yes

Because she checked to make sure that
you didn't have a game

Great

I can't wait

I can hear your sarcasm through the phone

Sorry

You know how much they grate on me

I know

We'll go and make nice and do what they
want then we can leave

And maybe do something more fun at
home 😉

The light at the end of the tunnel

When are you leaving for the rink?

Getting ready to head out now

Good luck!

You know I'll be watching

At home or from the shop?

Does it matter?

Declan: You answered my question

See if I cheer for you then 😜

I love you, Froggie

Don't wait up for me

I'll see you in the morning

Try and stop me from waiting up 😏

I smile at the lock screen on my phone—the picture of me and Alice kissing over the Cup with her flowers in the bowl. It's a touch blurry, but I don't care.

It's the two of us in a nutshell.

Hockey and flowers.

God, it makes me miss her even more. The bus pulls out from the hotel as I settle back into my seat. It's the last game on our West Coast road trip and I can't fucking wait to get home.

Road trips never used to bother me in the past.

Now? I hate being away from Alice.

I'm not new to relationships. I've had them in the past while playing. But I never had this burning need to get home.

Alice is the one that makes it hard to leave, but even sweeter to come home to.

"You look happy," Nick says from across the aisle.

"Ready to get home tonight."

"Do you miss Alice?"

I nod. "Yeah. You're lucky that Bex comes to all the games with us."

He blushes. He never likes the subject of Bex coming up if he can help it, always shy when discussing the subject.

"It's not like we get to spend all that much time together."

"Better than nothing," I point out.

If I'm not talking with Alice, I'm either thinking about

her or out on the ice. I wish I could talk to the guys about what I could do for Alice to convince her to stay married to me, but I can't. Sure, they might know that what we're doing is for the team, but they don't know the other part. About the trust.

If that got out, I don't know what would happen to Alice.

Fuck. She is the only person that matters. I don't want anything to happen to her because of this, and I don't want her parents finding out the truth behind our marriage.

Pushing them from the back of my mind, I turn my focus back to the game. Vancouver is a good team and my guys need my attention.

Because I'm ready to get a win on the board and head home to my wife.

THE HORN SOUNDS as Seattle pulls ahead. They really are a good fucking team. They're up 3-2 in the middle of the third. The home crowd is on their feet, celebrating the goal.

"Damn it."

I take a swig from my water bottle before hopping over the boards to take my position on the ice for the puck drop.

"Only one goal," Cash says. "We've got this."

"Damn right we do. We're not ending the trip on a loss."

The puck drops and our center sends it to me. My skates dig into the ice as I make my way over the blue line. Cash is neck and neck with me.

I shoot the puck his way before the defenseman collides with me.

"Shit."

I fall to the ice in a pile before trying to push my way back up. Their goalie has blocked the shot and they're taking off toward Nick.

Even from here, as I'm driving toward the action, I can see he's ready. He doesn't let them score. He blocks the shot with ease as it sails off his stick. Cash scoops it up, and getting onside, the two of us work together down the ice.

He passes the puck to me. I skate around one of their guys, and with no one in front of me but the goalie, I fire it —smack into the back of the net.

"Yes!"

Tied, 3-3.

"Great job, Paddy." Cash claps me on the shoulder. "One more and we've got this in the bag."

Coach Barney changes the line and I skate back over to the bench. The goal quiets the home crowd, giving us the momentum.

Troy is on fire tonight as he gets the puck and is on a tear toward their goalie. He dekes them out with ease and gets another fast goal.

"Yes!" I pump my fist in excitement.

We're only up by one, so we can't rest on our laurels now. With only five minutes left, it's a fight until the very end.

Shot upon shot is taken on goal with nothing going in. Each goalie is on top of their game. Nick is a beast between the pipes, not letting the pressure get to him.

With one minute to go, Vancouver pulls their goalie, giving themselves an extra man. Cash and I hit the ice.

They're swarming, but we're on them. They shoot the puck, but Nick swats the puck away with his stick, but Vancouver gets it and takes another shot. I block it before it can go in.

The final horn sounds as I fall to the ice with the puck ricocheting off of me.

Thank fuck.

"Hell, yeah, man!" Cash extends a hand, pulling me up and off the ice.

"You know, you didn't have to use your body to stop the goal," Nick says, taking off his helmet.

"I wasn't going to be the reason we went into overtime. Gotta help the team." I shrug.

Shaking hands with the Seattle players, I skate off the ice and answer the post-game questions by the awaiting media. It's all rote.

Playing together as a team.

Working hard to help us win.

Seattle is a good opponent.

By the time I'm out of my gear, Coach is congratulating us on the win and letting us know practice tomorrow is canceled in favor of a rest day.

Even better.

Grabbing my towel, I head to take a quick shower. I'm ready to get the hell home. When I get back to my locker, I grab my phone.

It's lit up with texts from Alice.

FROGGIE

That was an insane goal!!

Yeah!

Okay, c'mon

You guys got this

That block!

YES!

YOU WON!

Next time, can you make it easier on us?

That was way too stressful

I SMILE as I type out a quick response.

DECLAN

Sorry, Froggie

Next time, we'll try and score ten goals in the first period to put it away early

I would like that

But that goal!

Declan, that was amazing!

Thanks

Not even the best part of my night

Oh yeah?

What would that be?

Getting to crawl into bed next to you when I get home

I'll be waiting 🤍

I CAN'T WAIT to get home to Alice.

Chapter Twenty-Eight

ALICE

"Did your mom say why your dad wanted us to come over for dinner?"

Declan adjusts his tie, making sure it's perfectly in place.

"I don't know. She didn't say. Only that we had to join them for dinner and that they knew your schedule and knew you didn't have a game."

I clasp the pearl necklace and give myself another look in the mirror.

The black shift dress hits right below my knees, paired with sensible heels. My hair is curled. I don't look anything like I usually do.

Messy bun with overalls and white tennis shoes. That's where I'm most comfortable. Not going to a stuffy dinner with my parents.

"You know it's going to be okay, right?"

Declan wraps his arms around me, resting his chin on my shoulder, staring at me in the mirror. It helps to calm my nerves.

"Why can't my parents be more like your parents?"

He laughs, breath ghosting my cheek. "We all aren't that lucky."

"At least they like me."

"Oh, they love you probably more than they love me."

"At least someone's parents love me." I sigh.

"I'm sure they love you. Deep, deep, *deep* down," Declan says.

"Might as well get it over with."

I press a kiss to his lips, and we head out of his—*our*—room and leave for dinner.

Declan offers to drive, but I decline. I need to focus on the drive through the city to keep my nerves at bay. I wish the thought of a meal with my parents didn't stir up these feelings, but it does.

Declan's hand stays firmly on my leg the entire way over. His thumb rubs soothing circles against my knee.

Pulling into the gated community, he gives me a squeeze. "We'll be in, eat, and then leave. No lingering, okay?"

I smile at him as the iron gates swing open. "Still too long."

The house looms ahead as I park the car in the circular drive. Flipping down the visor, I check one last time to make sure my makeup is pristine. I don't need to give these two any ammunition to criticize me.

"You look great," Declan says, smiling at me. "Just relax, Froggie. I'm with you."

That sets me at ease. "Thanks."

"You and I can make it through anything together."

I blow out a breath. "All right, let's get this over with."

Getting out of the car, we link hands and walk up to the front door and I ring the bell. Their butler opens the door and welcomes us in.

"Good evening, Ms. Alice. Mr. Paddack."

"Hello." I give him a small nod.

"Your parents are in the study."

"Thank you." I swallow down the nerves that are threatening to take over. I walk the well-known path to where they're waiting. Before pushing the door open, Declan gives me another reassuring look.

"Alice. Declan. How are you?" Mom asks, standing from the couch.

"I'm fine," I say. It's a rote answer and not how I'm actually doing. It's not like I would ever tell her I'm nervous as hell to be here. Her coming to the shop the other day and now this? It all feels a little too much.

"Mr. Burke. It's nice to see you." Declan drops my hand to walk over and shake Dad's.

"The Black Diamonds are looking good this year," he tells him.

"Well, we have a good team," he agrees, stuffing his hands in his pockets. "It's been fun getting to play for them."

"Hopefully another trade isn't in your future."

"Dad," I scoff. "Don't say that."

He eyes me, like he can't believe I spoke to him like that.

"He's a professional athlete, Alice. It can happen at any time."

"Hopefully it won't," Declan says.

"I think he's proven himself to the team," I defend.

"And all it would take is one injury to end your career. I hope you're investing wisely," Dad tells him.

I shake my head. Of course this is my dad's biggest concern.

"Can I get a glass of wine while we wait for dinner?" I ask.

Dad shakes his head. "Dinner is already ready."

"It is?" I ask.

The hair on my arms stands on end. If there's one thing I know about my parents, it's that there is always time for a cocktail. How else would they look down their noses on people? Namely, me.

"Yes. We have some things to discuss with you." Dad gives me a pointed look before glancing at Declan. "With *both* of you."

My parents both head into the dining room together. It seems my feet are glued to the hardwood floors.

"You okay?" Declan whispers.

"Not even close."

"I'm here."

I try to give him a reassuring look, but based on the pinch between his brows, I don't convey it.

Walking into the dining room, plates are already set up. Mom takes her seat next to Dad, who sits at the head of the table. We take the two seats opposite Mom.

Mashed potatoes and peas. Chicken. Nothing overly fancy, but I'm going to have to feign interest in eating because I don't think I can swallow down anything.

"Are you going to tell us why you had us join you tonight?" I ask.

Taking the napkin and laying it across my lap, I grab my fork and push my peas around.

"Where are your manners, Alice?" Mom snaps. "You don't start conversations like that. Have we taught you nothing?"

They clearly have because I don't roll my eyes at them.

"You said you had something you wanted to discuss with us, and I can't help wondering what that might be."

Dad shakes his head. "We'll finish dinner first and then have a conversation."

I squeeze the fork in my hand tighter, the metal digging into my palm.

Anger and nerves are mixing together inside of me. I have no idea what my dad is playing at right now, but it's doing nothing to help.

Declan makes polite conversation with my dad as I cut into the chicken sitting on my plate. I pop a few bites, but it all feels like cement going down.

I push peas around on my plate and attempt to make it look like I'm actually eating.

"Alice, is there a reason you're not eating your dinner?" Mom asks, giving me a questioning look.

"I'm not all that hungry," I say.

"Alice, if you're going to act like this, we might as well just get this conversation over with." Dad wipes his mouth and throws his napkin down on the table.

I want to fire back at him. *How am I acting? You're the one that's being weird about what conversation we're supposedly having.*

"Can you tell me what it is we need to discuss? You're the one that told us to come over tonight."

I fold my hands in my lap and turn to give my father my full attention.

Instead of diving into it, he walks into the study and comes back with a manila folder in his hand.

"Care to explain this?"

He slide the thick envelope over to me and I undo the clasp. Pulling out the papers, my jaw drops in shock.

"What is this?"

"Proof that your marriage is a sham."

"What?" Declan leans over my shoulder to look at the stack of papers.

"Do you really think we wouldn't do our due diligence?" Dad asks. I hate that my eyes match his at this very moment.

They are full of disappointment. It's not the first time I've seen him look at me like this, but it stings, nonetheless.

"Where did you get these?"

A copy of our marriage certificate. Pictures from our social media—Declan with another woman, me with another man. Pictures from my dating profile that I had set up earlier this year.

"You were set to inherit a large sum of money, Alice. Imagine my surprise when you show up and happen to be married. It was questionable at best. You would be coming into your trust under false pretenses."

"What do you mean false pretenses? We got married."

Dad scoffs. "In Vegas. When you were drunk, based on the photos."

Of course he has pictures from when we were there. Sure, we were drinking, but we don't look trashed in any of the photos.

"Is this even a real relationship?" Dad asks. "Are you even in love? Were you even dating?"

Ice slides down my throat, settling in my stomach. I can't believe what I'm looking at. My eyes flit up to stare at my parents. At the two people who are supposed to love me unconditionally.

It's like I don't even know them.

"Is this really how much you hate me? That you're willing to void my trust to try and keep me under your thumb?"

Mom bristles at the comment. "We certainly don't hate you, Alice."

"You might not, but you don't love me or care. And I'm not sure which is worse." I sigh.

"We can—"

"No." I interrupt Declan. "The fact that you what, did all of this so I'd go and work for Dad?"

"Alice, we've put up with your childish dreams long enough. Working in a flower shop? It's not what Burkes do. It's not a *suitable* position."

"It's what this Burke wants to do."

"You won't do it with your grandfather's money," Dad states.

"Unbelievable." I shake my head.

"Doesn't it really matter what Alice wants to do?" Declan asks.

"Declan, no. Stop."

"No. Why do they get to dictate what you do?"

"What if one of our friends saw her?" Mom looks appalled, like this is the worst thing that could happen.

Dad nods in agreement. "Our name carries a lot of weight in this city. I don't want people thinking less of us because of you."

"Because I have a good job that lets me save and pay the bills?"

"You can't possibly be saving that much money," Mom says.

"You don't have any idea how much I make because you've never bothered to take an interest in what I do."

"You're an associate at a flower shop."

"One that I'm hoping to buy," I fire back at her.

"What?" I don't think I've ever seen my Dad's face turn so red. "Is that what you were going to use the trust for?"

Disdain drips from his voice.

"Yes," I answer. "It's what I've always wanted to do."

"It's not what Burkes do."

"I don't care. I don't want to work for you." I push all the papers back toward him.

"Then if you can save money, you'll be buying it yourself. I've already sent this to the estate lawyers, and you will not be getting one cent of your trust."

"You two are unbelievable. Treating your only daughter like this? I'm not stealing your money. I'm doing what I'm passionate about. What I've always wanted to do."

"Alice, work for your father," Mom says. "You'll make more money than you could ever dream of."

"And be miserable."

"Happiness is overrated," she says.

"Not for me."

Throwing my napkin down on my plate, I watch as a few peas roll off onto the neatly pressed table cloth. I don't care. I don't care that I shouldn't leave the table until I'm excused. I'm tired of trying to fit in the perfect little image that these two have of me. I tell them as much.

"You know what? I'm done. I'm done trying to be the perfect daughter and live up to some imaginary standard of what you think I need to be. You can have the money. If it means I have to be someone I'm not, I don't want it. I don't want to be a part of this family anymore."

"Alice. You will not talk to us like that," Dad snaps.

I stand while Declan is still sitting, completely stunned at everything I'm saying.

"It's a good thing I don't care then." I hold out my hand for Declan. "C'mon. Let's go."

"That's it? You're leaving?" Mom asks, her own reaction matching Declan's.

"Yes." I look at both of them. "You've made it perfectly clear that unless I bend to your every whim, I don't have a place here in this family. I'm leaving. Declan and I are leaving. I'm done. Until you two decide that what I do is valuable and meaningful *to me*, then I don't think we have anything to say to one another."

"Alice!" Mom shrieks as I leave the dining room, Declan hot on my heels. "You can't just walk out like that."

"Oh, yeah? Watch me."

Chapter Twenty-Nine

I've never seen Alice like this. She's shaking. Physically shaking after the conversation with her parents.

If she weren't my primary concern, I'd march right back into the dining room and tell her parents what I really think of them.

How can two people treat the best person I know like that? Like she is nothing more than a staff member of theirs to control with the purse strings.

"Want me to drive?" I ask as soon as the front door shuts behind us.

"No." Alice's voice is clipped. "I'm fine."

Fine. Yeah, right. That's a lie if I've ever heard one.

"Okay."

She opens the driver's side door and slides in, slamming it shut with more force than necessary.

Shit. This isn't good.

In all the years I've known her, I don't think I've ever seen her mad. It's something I know she learned from her upbringing—never to show emotion.

But right now? Her knuckles are white as they grip the

steering wheel. Her eyes are focused on the road ahead. She's mumbling to herself as she exits the neighborhood.

I don't take my eyes off her as she heads back to our place.

I can't believe her parents did that. Went through all that trouble just so Alice wouldn't inherit her trust and would go work for them.

I'm angry, but right now, I'm pushing that to the side because all I can think about is Alice and how upset she is.

"Do you want a milkshake?" she asks, putting on her blinker and turning into the parking lot of a local ice cream shop.

"Sure."

At this point, she could ask if I wanted a pet giraffe and I'd say yes to keep her from getting more upset.

"Chocolate strawberry swirl and a vanilla bean caramel shake, please," she tells the speaker.

"Here." I pull my wallet out from my pocket and hand over my credit card. "I'll buy them."

That turns her ire on me. "I can afford milkshakes."

"I wasn't saying you couldn't. You drove; the least I can do is buy us our shakes."

Alice doesn't say another word before grabbing the card in my hand and driving up to the window to hand it over to the cashier.

He hands over two Styrofoam cups and straws and Alice hands the chocolate one to me before tearing open her straw and stabbing it through the rounded plastic lid of her shake. Turning onto our street, seeing our house, pulls a sigh of relief from me.

Maybe Alice will actually talk to me now.

But that's wishful thinking as she parks the car and walks into the house. Her footfalls are heavy as she kicks off her heels and rips the clip out of her hair.

Undoing my tie, I watch as she paces around the kitchen. I take one of the barstools, sucking on my drink as she keeps moving.

I don't know how much time has passed, but I'm worried. Even more so now because she hasn't said a word. Just drinking her stupid milkshake and muttering to herself.

When she slurps down the last dregs, she slams the empty cup on the counter.

When she turns to face me, tears wet her eyes. "Why are they like this? How could two people who raised me care so little about me that they'd go through the trouble of finding a way to void my trust?"

I fly out of my barstool and wrap my arms around her, squeezing her tight. I pour every ounce of love I have for this woman into the hug.

"I'm sorry." It's all I can say, running my fingers through her hair. "I wish there was something I could do."

"I hate this. All because I never wanted to work for the family business."

Pulling her back, I wipe the tears from her cheeks. Her blue eyes are red rimmed and it breaks my heart.

"They don't deserve someone as good as you."

"Maybe if they had a son, it wouldn't matter. Someone they could groom like they couldn't me." She pause for a moment, then continues, "Declan…"

"What, Froggie?"

"What's going to happen? Do you think they're going to out us?"

"Do you really think they'd be that cruel?"

"I didn't think they'd stoop so low as to do what they did tonight, but they proved me wrong." She brushes a tear away with anger.

"If it happens, if people start snooping about our relationship in the press, we'll deal with it."

"But—"

I cut her off with a kiss. "It doesn't matter, Alice. We'll tell them we're in love. That it just made sense. I don't care what anyone says."

I love this woman and will do anything to prove it.

"I think…"

"What?" I tip her chin up to look at me.

"I need to lie down. I'm exhausted."

"Want to put on a movie and curl up on the couch?"

That earns me a small smile. "Will you rub my head for me?"

"Anything. Anything you want, Froggie."

I chuckle to myself the minute she walks into the living room and turns on an action movie. I should have known.

Dropping down next to her, I nestle a pillow under her head and run my fingers through her hair, massaging her scalp. She burrows as close as possible to me.

Fuck.

This night took a turn I wasn't expecting. Even with the crash bangs echoing around the house, I can hear her soft sniffles.

Fuck. I hate her parents. Hate that they didn't come to our college graduation. Hate that they've always made her feel less than. This beautiful, perfect woman that I love solely because she exists.

My phone buzzes in my pocket, a reminder that we have an early practice tomorrow.

Shit.

I wish I could call in sick and spend the day with Alice. Make sure she's okay. I love what I do. I love getting to be a professional hockey player. But right now? I fucking hate it.

If I can't be here for Alice, I'll get others who can.

Chapter Thirty

"Hey. You awake?" Declan whispers.

I nod, not moving. He's curled around me, his body heat warming me from the outside in.

I spent most of the night tossing and turning. Declan turned in early because of practice today, but I stayed on the couch until two, not wanting to keep him awake.

When I finally went to bed, Declan pulled me into him and didn't let me out of his hold.

At least someone cares about me.

"I have to get ready for practice."

"I know."

"Are you going to be okay?" Declan asks, cupping my cheek and turning my attention to him.

"I'll be fine."

"You don't have to pretend," he says. "I know you're not."

"No, but I'll be fine while you're at practice. I promise."

"You sure?"

I nod, turning back over.

"I let Leon know you wouldn't be in today."

"You did?"

"Yes. Stay home. Just…" He brushes a piece of hair out of my face. "Let me know if you need anything, okay?"

"I will."

Declan presses a kiss to my cheek as he hops out of bed, taking his warmth with him.

The sun is starting to peek through the closed blinds, casting long shadows across the room.

My mind is a chaotic mess after last night. It's not that I lost my trust. Fine. Whatever. I've been saving every penny since I started working at Enchanted Petals because I love it so much and wanted to take over. Leon always talked about his dream of passing it on to me so he could retire early to enjoy his life with Jacob.

No.

It's the fact that my parents care so little about me that they'd go through the trouble of nullifying my trust just to keep me under their thumb.

Did they really think I'd give up everything *I've* wanted since I graduated from college and started working?

Hurt and anger battle for control as Declan drops one last kiss to my cheek before leaving.

I have no idea how long I stay here. Exhaustion clings to me, but I can't stay like this all day.

When the stream of sunlight brightens, I know I need to get up. Glancing at the clock, it's well after one in the afternoon.

Piling my hair on top of my head, I throw on one of Declan's sweatshirts over my sleep shorts and tank and pad into the kitchen.

Maybe a cup of coffee will help me feel better. At least

give me a clear head so I can try to come up with a plan of action going forward.

But before I can do anything, the front door swings open.

"Alice?"

"Kathleen? What are you doing here?"

My jaw drops in shock as Declan's parents stride in through the front door.

"Oh, sweetheart." Kathleen walks around the counter and pulls me in for a hug. The smell of lavender invades my senses, causing tears to well in my eyes. "Declan told us what happened."

"Did you drive all night?"

"We got up early this morning to drive. You know it's not that bad without traffic."

"You didn't need to come." Except I squeeze her tighter to me.

"Nonsense. I whipped up some soup for you and you are going to sit and eat it until you feel better."

"Excuse me," Aiden interjects, shutting the door behind him. "Who made the soup?"

Kathleen untangles her arms from mine and pats my cheek. "Fine. He made the soup. But I told him we had to do it."

"Like I wouldn't have done it." Aiden sidles up to us with a smile on his face. "She thinks that she knows everything, but you know we'd do anything for you, Alice. You're like a daughter to us."

I can't hold back the tears. A fresh wave roll down my cheeks as I try to wipe them away, but to no avail.

"Oh, sweetheart." Kathleen pulls me in again, rubbing circles on my back as I let the tears go. "I'm so sorry."

I can't say anything. My throat is too thick with emotion.

"I know your parents were shitheads to you—"

Aiden is interrupted almost immediately.

"You can't say that to her right now," Kathleen hisses.

He shrugs as I turn to face him.

"As I was saying. I know your parents were terrible to you and basically disowned you, but if you're looking for a set of adopted parents, you have us. We might cuss, drink a lot, and drop in unannounced, but we do it because we care."

"I'd take the two of you any day," I say, pulling Declan's dad in for a hug.

"Good. Now, time to eat some soup." Kathleen steers me toward the kitchen right as the doorbell rings. "Aiden. Get that."

I laugh as he gripes but does exactly what she says. Leon and Jacob are at the door with a stunning bouquet in hand.

"Okay, did Declan call everyone?" I throw my hands up, leaning back in the barstool.

They shed their coats, hanging them on the hook and toeing off their shoes.

"When I got his text this morning, I knew things were bad," Leon says. "He was worried, and so am I."

"I told him I was fine."

Jacob waves me off, grabbing one of my vases to put the flowers in. "I'd be worried if you were."

"I'm going to have to have a talk with him about what fine means."

Aiden pats me on the back as he goes over toward the stove. "Then he knows exactly what it means. Fine is never fine."

A glass of amber liquid is slid in front of me. Jacob winks as he takes a seat next to me. "Agreed. You found a good one."

"Yeah, I really did." I swirl the glass around before taking a sip.

The bourbon burns on the way down, but helps to settle my insides. Leon is at the stove, helping Kathleen with the soup while Aiden turns the oven on to heat up the bag of rolls he brought.

All these people are here because of Declan. Because of the one person that means more to me than anything else.

Who cares so much about me that he didn't want me left to my own devices today. His parents drove over eight hours to be here. I know Leon closed the shop because without a manager there, who else would oversee things?

My parents might be the worst and not care, but Declan does.

My husband, who I love more than anything in the world, even though we got married on a whim in Vegas.

I don't give a damn that I lost my trust.

I have Declan and these people.

That means more than they'll ever know.

"You look sad," Leon says, leaning across the counter at me. "You had a smile and now it's gone."

My lip quivers. "I wish I could buy the shop from you, but I don't think I'll be able to now." It sinks like a lead weight in my stomach. All I've ever wanted is now out of reach.

"Why would you think that?" Leon asks, looking confused.

"You told me that." I point out. "You wanted to sell Enchanted Petals free and clear so you could travel with Jacob."

Jacob nods his head next to me. "Darling, you've said that several times."

"I have?" Leon looks chagrined. "I'm sorry if I made

you think that's the only way you could have the shop. The only person I trust with my baby is you."

"Hey!" Jacob interjects. "I thought I was your baby."

I snicker at the two of them, the lightness clearing my full head.

"Of course you are," Leon tells him. "But I've had Enchanted Petals much longer than you, and I love it. I wanted to make sure it was in good hands. Alice is the only person I would sell it to."

"Which is impossible because my parents voided my trust."

"We can work something else out, Alice," Leon says.

"Really?"

Leon cups my cheeks, forcing my eyes to meet his. "Yes. I want you to have the store. There is no one that loves it more than you, and I'm including myself in that. You have a passion for what you do that shines through in everything you create. Clients love you. Customers love you. I love you. It's a done deal."

"You mean that? You're not just saying it?" It's been a roller coaster of emotions these last eighteen hours. The last thing I want is to get my hopes up to have them dashed.

"Of course."

"I really want to be more excited right now, but with everything else going on, it's hard," I confess.

Leon kisses my cheek and Jacob pats my knee. "Take a few days to get your head on straight. We'll worry about ironing out the details later."

"Which means it's time to eat," Aiden says. "We made enough to feed an army, so I hope you're hungry."

"I'm starving," Leon says.

As everyone heads into the dining room, I pop off the stool and go to grab my phone, firing off a text to Declan.

. . .

ALICE

You didn't need to call in reinforcements

DECLAN

Yes I did

I was worried about you

As much as I said I didn't need anyone, I'm glad they're here

Good

I should be home soon

I love you

Not as much as I love you, Froggie

WITH EVERYONE AT THE TABLE, noise fills the house. It helps to make the ache in my chest go away.

Because while my family by blood don't want anything to do with me unless I live up to their vision of a good daughter, but these people? They love me for me.

I don't know if I'll ever be able to tell them that. But I'll keep them around for as long as they'll let me.

Chapter Thirty-One

ALICE

DECLAN

Are you sure you're good for tonight?

No one would blame you if you wanted to
stay home

ALICE

I promise

I'm okay

If I had any issues going to the game
tonight, I would tell you

Okay, you know I'm just worried about you

I love you for it

But I'm good

Okay

See you after?

Nothing could stop me

Taking the elevator up to the family suite, my stomach feels like a lead weight. I'm not nervous for the game or spending the evening with the girls, but I'm still trying to come to terms with everything that's happened over the last few days. When my parents called us over for dinner, I didn't plan on the worst happening. But them invalidating my trust?

I shake my head, walking toward the suite. I still can't believe it.

But then Leon swooped in and told me Enchanted Petals is all but mine, and I've been a mess of emotions since. The easy thing to do would be to hide away and let everything overwhelm me. It's *not* what I'm going to do. It wouldn't do me any good.

I hear familiar voices as I cross the threshold into the suite. Angie and Piper are standing there, and the moment they see me, they hurry over to wrap me in a hug.

I guess that answers the question of whether they know what happened.

"How are you?" Piper asks. "Cash filled me in."

"Yeah. I can't believe what your parents did," Angie says.

"Should I be worried on how gossipy the guys are?"

Piper pulls back and smiles at me. "Those boys don't know how to keep anything to themselves."

The diamond ring glints on her finger in the harsh overhead light.

"You got that right. But it's because they love us," Piper says.

"Is it okay they told us?" Angie asks.

I nod. "He's only looking out for me." I shrug a shoulder. "It's kind of nice to have people in my corner."

Angie smiles, wrapping an arm around my shoulder.

"You're part of the Black Diamonds family now. You both are. So whatever you need, just tell us. We're here for you."

My chin quivers as I pull them both back in for hugs. "You have no idea how much that means to me."

"I'm sorry for everything you're going through," Angie says, leading us toward the seats.

"I don't want to talk about it. It's going to make me emotional and it's the last thing I want."

"You got it." Piper drops down into the seat next to me, patting my knee.

Tonight the only thing I want to enjoy is watching my husband play hockey, with friends around me who have turned into family. These women not only welcomed me, but their partners welcomed Declan into the fold. I can't imagine how hard it is to get traded this far into your career, but Declan took it all in stride.

I don't know what I'd do without him. Without these women. It has me smiling for the first time in days. Because while I might have lost one family, I gained another.

Cheers start to ring out around the arena as the guys take the ice. Even though it's still early, everyone is excited for this season.

The hockey game tonight is the just the distraction I need. They are playing Detroit who, as Declan says, is one of the worst teams in the league besides the Knights. It's easy to see the unmatched skill as the two teams take each other on.

Troy is able to get an easy goal right away, and Nick defends our goal, blocking the only early shot they are able to send his way. Cash and Declan are a force to be reckoned with, as Cash passes to Declan who gets a goal.

"Hell, yeah!" I jump up and down, screaming with the rest of the arena. "That's my man!"

"Damn right." Piper wraps an arm around me. "Great assist, Cash!"

"I'm going to go grab a drink. You two want anything?"

"I'm good."

"I'll get something later."

I nod, walking back to the kitchenette to grab myself a beer. I crack it open with a hiss and take a cooling sip. My phone buzzes in my pocket.

Pulling it out, I see an email from my father's attorney. He would be the only one to have an attorney working on the weekend. I roll my eyes at him.

My teeth crack as I grind them together. He couldn't have waited until Monday to tell me that my trust is voided for falsifying my relationship?

God, what a dick.

Why in the world did they even have kids if this is how they are going to treat their offspring? Maybe if I were a man and he could have molded me into his perfect little soldier, he might have something other than contempt for me. I've never gotten love or care. Feigned interest and contempt on a good day.

"Sorry, Dad. I don't want your job," I mutter, locking my phone and putting it face down on the counter.

Someone I don't know is grabbing a plate of meatballs and smiles at me. I return it, trying not to look crazed by talking to myself.

Three short bursts vibrate my phone against the marble. I should turn the damn thing off if it's going to keep doing that. The crowd starts cheering. My guess is it was a good stop since I don't hear the siren indicating a goal.

Glancing at my phone, there are three messages from Leon.

LEON

Hey, babe

Here's the contract I've drawn up for
Enchanted Petals

No rush. I know you're at the game with
that sexy husband of yours

I ROLL my eyes as I read his message. I'm not surprised he
says this. Tapping on his message, I pull up his contract.
Looking it over, all the terms and conditions are laid out.

Except one thing.

ALICE

Are you giving me Enchanted Petals for
free?

No

Then why don't I see anything about
payment?

It's taken care of

Taken care of?

How?

Who took care of it?

I plead the fifth

Ugh!

I've had enough surprises this week

> Why don't you ask that sexy husband of yours 😏💦

> Have you two been conspiring behind my back?

> I wouldn't call it conspiring

> Helping you, maybe

> Now, go watch that husband of yours play hockey for both of us

> Please

> You're just watching it because you're obsessed with hockey butts

> Duh

> Who isn't?!

"EVERYTHING OKAY BACK HERE?"

Piper startles me, and I drop my phone on the counter. "Yeah. It's good."

"You were gone for a while, so I wanted to check and make sure you're alright."

"Just my husband conspiring behind my back to start the process of buying Enchanted Petals."

I slide my phone into the back pocket of my jeans.

"Wait, seriously?"

I nod. Leon and I started the topic of me buying him out this past week, but apparently he and Declan started the ball rolling.

"I can't believe them."

"It's nice that they both care about you so much," Piper says.

"It is. Now to figure out a way to pay Declan back."

I have a good chunk in savings, but even then, it was still going to stretch me to drum up the cash to start the buyout process.

Since I've been doing the books, I know exactly how much the shop is making. Comparing it quarter to quarter, I can see just exactly what the event with the Black Diamonds got us. A huge boost that hasn't quit ever since.

"Well," Piper says, grabbing a fresh drink and handing one off to me, "it's better than him not caring, right?"

"You're right. God, I love that man."

"Yeah, you two are pretty cute together. I'd say he's a keeper."

"He is."

I follow her back to our seats just as Troy goes on a breakaway and puts the puck in the back of the net.

Damn. The team is on fire tonight. I high-five Angie and take my seat.

"Team's looking really good this year. Is it always this fun watching them play?"

"Yes." They both answer immediately.

"It's even more fun after," Piper says, waggling her eyebrows.

"Piper, we're in public," Angie hisses.

"What?" She throws her hands up. "It's not like you weren't thinking it."

"I think we all were." I giggle.

It's not like Declan and I were together when he used to play for the Knights, but I could always hear how dejected he was when they lost, which was more often than not. Every time he walks through the door, he's beaming. You can't erase his smile. He's downright giddy.

I love seeing him so happy.

"In case Declan didn't tell you," Angie starts as the

horn to signify the end of the period sounds, "we're all going out after the game. And you're not allowed to say no."

"Right. There will be plenty of time for shenanigans tonight," Piper says. "I like the afternoon games."

"Me too," Angie says. "Is Puck taken care of?"

Piper nods. "One of the neighborhood kids comes over to check on him and feed him."

"Oh, I bet he loves that." I smile.

"Puck loves anyone who will give him attention. And the kid is really sweet. He's saving his money to go to math camp this spring."

"That's really kind," I say.

"Yeah, Cash is a good guy." Her eyes are focused on the bench as Cash and the rest of the team head to the locker room for intermission. "What the kid doesn't know is Cash has already given his mom the money to send him, so it's going to be fun money for him."

"I love that."

I remember Cash's reputation from a few years ago all too well. The bad boy of the league. Hearing him now? You would never know that guy existed.

"Good thing he's a keeper," Angie says.

I laugh since she wasn't around to hear our earlier conversation.

"I'm not giving that man back for anything." She stares down at her ring. "I still can't believe he kept the proposal a secret."

"Oh, I can," Angie states. "I was in on it and it was hard. You're too sneaky for your own good."

"I am not!" Piper scoffs. "Am I?"

She turns her attention to me.

"Umm."

Piper waves me off. "It doesn't matter. All that matters is we're engaged."

I fiddle with the gold band on my ring finger. I don't have anything like Piper or Angie, but I don't care. The simple band is all I need.

It's perfect for me and Declan. Perfect for working at the shop.

I don't need anything fancier because as long as I have Declan?

I'll have everything I need in life.

Chapter Thirty-Two

DECLAN

My eyes lock onto Alice's the minute I step foot into the family room after the game. Her smile is wide as she spots me and darts over.

"Hey Froggie, enjoy the game?"

"Looked pretty good out there."

"What can I say? I want to impress my wife."

She presses up onto her toes, lips brushing against mine.

"I have to say watching you play is hot."

"I do like hearing that." I link my hands behind her back and hold her close, dropping my forehead to hers. "Did you have fun with the girls?"

"I did. We're all going out tonight."

"We are?" I ask.

She nods. "Yeah."

"Damn. There go the plans I had for us." I waggle my brows at her.

"Declan." She smacks me in the chest. "We can go out and celebrate your win and have a few drinks.

"Alright, alright." I steal another kiss from her.

Grabbing her hand, I wave goodbye to the guys as we head out of the arena. We have one more home game this week before we have a short stint on the road down in Dallas.

Thank God.

I don't want to be away from Alice right now.

She says she's okay, but I'm still worried. The pain flashes across her face when she thinks I'm not looking. But who wouldn't still be affected when your parents treat you like that?

"Hey." Alice squeezes my bicep. "You okay?"

I beep my key fob to my truck and toss my bag into the backseat.

"I'm good, why?"

"You're more quiet than usual."

"Sorry. I have a few things on my mind."

"Like how you won the game?"

"Among other things," I say.

"That should be the only thing on your mind. You kicked ass tonight."

"Like I said, I want to impress my wife."

"You never have to impress me. I think you're a pretty impressive person as is."

"Oh, yeah? Would you care to come home with me and tell me just how impressive you do find me?"

She shakes her head. "We're going out with our friends. Then we can do whatever we want, okay?"

"Fine. But not too late, because I know you have a long week at the shop."

Shock colors her features. "I just remembered I have a bone to pick with you."

I go to open the door for her, but she stops me, resting her hip against the door and crossing her arms.

"Me? What did I do?"

On the long list of people who have wronged her, I don't know how I register.

"I got a text from Leon saying he has a draft of the contract for the store."

Oh, shit.

"Oh, you did?"

Yeah, I'm definitely at the top of her list at the moment.

"Don't you play coy with me, Declan Paddack. I've known you for too long and it's not a good look."

"Before you get going—"

She cuts me off with a brisk kiss. That I was not expecting.

"Is that a good thing?" I ask.

"Yes. Why did you not tell me?"

"Because Leon wasn't supposed to tell you until next week after I talked to you. But it's only the first payment. I know it's bigger than you expected, and I didn't want you to have to worry about anything. Put your savings toward future payments, but I want you to have Enchanted Petals sooner rather than later."

"How can I argue with that?"

"I really thought you were going to lay into me."

"I still might." She fists the lapels of my suit jacket. "Definitely Leon."

"Leon was the one that wanted something in place as quickly as possible. He wanted to make sure you knew that he wasn't going to back out."

"I didn't think he would."

"He cares about you, Froggie. We both do. You can't fault him for caring."

"You know what this means?" she asks, a smile spreading across her face.

"Tell me."

"That I'll be the owner of Enchanted Petals."

I match her smile, mine even bigger if possible. "It's what you've always wanted."

"I couldn't have done it without you."

"You're my wife, Alice. I would do anything for you."

"About that…"

A sinking feeling settles in my gut. I don't know where she's going with this, but after the week she's had, it's derailed my plan on asking her to make this permanent.

She starts fiddling with the buttons on my jacket, not looking at me.

"Froggie. What is it?" I knuckle her chin, tilting her gaze to meet mine.

Her blue eyes are a swarm of emotions.

"I know this thing was only supposed to be temporary."

"Right."

"Well, what if we made it…untemporary?"

"Untemporary? Like permanent?"

She shrugs a shoulder. "I mean, technically it's already real. But I mean permanent."

"So you don't want to end this right now?"

"Why would I want to end it?" she asks.

"Well, your dad figured it out and you're not getting your trust, so I was worried you'd bail."

Alice shakes her head. "Declan, the very last thing I want is to end this thing with you."

Grabbing her ass, I lift her off the ground and push her against the side of the truck.

"The very last thing *I* want is for this thing to end. I was trying to come up with a way to talk to you about making it permanent, but then everything happened."

Her jaw ticks. "Things still feel really messy. I know I have a lot to work out with everything, but…"

"I don't care. You are the most important person to me, Froggie, and that's all that matters. Whatever you need from me to help heal from this, I'm here. No questions asked."

"I feel like you're signing on for a lot," she says.

"Don't care. You're *my wife*. If you want me to go yell at your parents, I'll do it. If you want me to drive you to see a therapist, I'll do it. Kickboxing? You name it, I'll do it."

"This. This is why I don't want this to end, Declan. You have my back in ways I never even knew I needed."

"Because I love you, Froggie."

"Say it again."

I press in closer, dropping my mouth over hers. "I love you, Alice. More than anything else in this world. All I want is you."

Her fingertips ghost over my lips. My cheeks. My nose. I feel her touch everywhere.

"You've always been my person, Declan. I love you. Maybe getting drunk in Vegas and getting married was the push you and I finally needed, but I've never been happier in my entire life."

"My wife really is smart."

She laughs. "Do you want to stay married because you like calling me your wife?"

"I mean, maybe."

"Is this what I have to look forward to for the rest of our lives?"

"Yes. Until forever." I nod. "Calling you my wife. Loving you. Supporting you. Giving you whatever you need, Alice, because I love you."

"I'll be pretty happy with forever too."

I kiss her. I don't care that we're in the middle of the team parking lot. Every part of me settles. Because this thing with Alice will never end.

No timelines. No deadlines. No quiet divorce after a year.

It's only the two of us. Husband and wife.

Together.

Forever.

Epilogue

"**A**re you nervous, Paddy?" Cash asks.

"Why would I be nervous?"

He shrugs a shoulder, adjusting his tie. "What if Alice decides she doesn't want to marry you?"

I roll my eyes at him as Troy slaps him on the back of the head.

"You do realize we're already married, right?" I ask him. "We're renewing our vows."

"Just making sure." Cash winks at me.

"Asshole," I mutter.

"Leave him alone," Troy says. "Angie just texted and said Alice is ready to get this show on the road."

I smile. "Of course she is."

If it had been up to me, we would have done this last summer after getting knocked out of the playoffs. But with Froggie taking over Enchanted Petals, there weren't enough hours in the day for her.

Now that things have settled down for her, and with a good team at the shop, I convinced her the time was right to renew our vows.

That, and my mother was going to kill me if she didn't get to see her only son's wedding.

Minor detail.

Dad pops his head inside the room. "Ready, Declan?"

I smooth a hand down the front of my tie. "Hell, yes."

He shakes his head. "Please don't cuss in front of your mother during the service. I'll never hear the end of it."

"Why would you never hear the end of it?" I ask.

"Because I didn't raise you *not* to cuss, so she'll blame me."

All the guys laugh, clapping me on the back as they start to head out. "Sorry, Dad. I'll try."

That ship has long since sailed, but if that's what my mom wants today, I'll try. For her, at least.

Following my dad through the house, I head through the doors to the back yard and stop dead in my tracks.

It's like the shop exploded in our yard. White roses line the aisle toward the gazebo where the guys and my dad wait, ready to marry the two of us again.

"Damn." I whistle, heading to the gazebo where swaths of fabric are draped over the wooden structure. Ranunculus and roses are mixed in together throughout it, matching the boutonniere pinned to my shirt. Twinkling lights finish it off.

Leon helped Alice get everything ready this morning. She didn't want to leave this up to anyone else but her.

It's fucking stunning.

Everyone is standing, waiting for Alice to come out. I try not to fidget. For someone who wanted to move things along, she sure is taking her time.

When the back doors open and the music starts, Alice takes my breath away.

The dress she's wearing is simple. The strapless dress

hits just above her knee, with lace flowers covering the fabric.

It's perfect for her. Her blonde hair flows in soft waves.

But the best part? The smile she's wearing as she walks toward me. It's one just for me. The one that I fall in love with more and more each day.

When she steps up to me, I can't help but sweep her into my arms and lay one on her.

"You're not supposed to kiss her until after!" Cash yells.

I smile down at the most beautiful woman in the world. "I'll kiss her whenever the hell I want."

"Really, Declan?" Mom sighs. "It's your wedding day."

"Sorry, Mom." I laugh, wiping the lipstick from my mouth.

"Are you two ready?" Dad asks.

Alice hands the bouquet to Leon before taking both of my hands.

"Ready," Alice says.

I squeeze her hands as Dad begins.

"Friends and family, we are here today to celebrate the love of Alice and Declan as they renew their wedding vows. They love each other so much, they couldn't wait to do it again."

Alice and I share a smile. More like we don't really remember the first time, but we're not telling them that.

He talks about love and commitment before turning to Alice. "You've both written your own vows. Alice, would you like to go first?"

She smiles at my dad, tears lining her bright, blue eyes.

"Declan, you're my favorite person in the whole world. From the minute I met you when I puked all over your shoes, we've been a team."

"Puking *and* cussing?" Mom groans. "We're going to have words, Declan."

"Kathleen!" Dad hisses.

"Right. Sorry. Not the time. Continue."

Alice laughs, shaking her head at them. "We've shared everything together since that night, and I wouldn't have it any other way. We've had our ups and downs, but you've been by my side through it all. You're my family. As long as I have you, Declan, I'll have everything I need in life. I love you."

I love you I mouth back to her.

"Declan?" Dad nods at me.

"Froggie, I love you more than life itself. I think I've loved you since the night we met, but it took me a few years to figure out what it meant. You're my biggest cheerleader and support me in every way imaginable. I know this life isn't easy, but there is no one else I'd want to do it with. Through the good and the bad, the wins and losses, we're in this together. I love you."

Alice wipes a stray tear from her cheek.

"Considering you already have rings and aren't exchanging new ones," Dad continues, "I can now pronounce you husband and wife. Again. You may kiss—"

I don't wait for him to finish as I cup Alice's cheeks and slant my mouth over hers. I pour every ounce of love I have for this woman into this kiss.

My best friend. The person I got so drunk with in Vegas, I don't remember marrying her.

My wife.

Cheers rain down on us before champagne is passed around as hugs are given out. As servers place trays of food on the tables, a few people head to the makeshift dance floor that sits in one corner of the yard.

"You two are so damn cute, I can't even handle it," Leon says.

"Thanks, Leon," Alice says, wrapping him in a hug.

"And thanks for looking after the shop next week so we can finally go on a honeymoon."

He shakes his head. "I can't believe Declan hasn't taken you anywhere before."

"Hey!" I interject. "It's not my fault that I can't pull her away."

Alice groans. "Not this again."

"I would've taken you to Fiji last year if you let me," I say.

"I thought you two were going to Hawaii?" Jacob asks, coming up beside Leon and passing over a drink.

"We are." I nod. "But I would take Alice anywhere."

"Hmm. Maybe we should go to Fiji once they get back," Leon says. "That sounds pretty nice."

"Scout it out and let us know," Alice says. "I don't want to be gone that long."

"Sounds like your husband isn't doing his job then." He waggles his brows at her.

"Okay, now I'm offended," I scoff.

"Trust me, he is more than doing his job." Alice winks at them.

"Damn, Froggie. I didn't think I'd ever hear you say something like that."

She laughs, grabbing two glasses of champagne. "I don't want them spreading any rumors."

"You really think they'd do that?"

She sips on her drink, nodding her head. "Of course they would. They're the biggest gossips, and we don't need Cash getting wind of that."

"He'd be insufferable."

As our friends and family take to the dance floor, I grab Alice's hand and pull her inside for a moment together. The first we've really had all day.

Her blue eyes are soft in the dark house, full of nothing but love.

"Any regrets?" I ask, tucking a lock of hair behind her ear.

She nods her head, causing a moment of panic to erupt in my stomach.

"Only that we didn't do this sooner."

"Way to bury the lede, Froggie." I breathe a sigh of relief. "You had me going for a minute there."

Alice wraps her arms around me, resting her chin on my chest. "Sorry. Do you need me to get you another drink?"

I shake my head, resting my forehead against hers. "No. Because I have a lot of things planned for tonight and I don't want to be too drunk to do them."

She bites down on her bottom lip. "You know…"

"What?"

"I think two of the best things in my life happened because I got drunk."

"Meeting me and getting married the first time?" I waggle my brows at her.

She nods. "Yeah."

"Do you plan on doing it a third time?"

"No. Because I want to remember everything about this night."

"We could always get really drunk again, forget it, and then renew our vows again."

She bursts out laughing. "We are not making this a thing, Declan."

"What's wrong with wanting to marry you over and over again, Froggie?"

"Twice is good enough for me. I'm not going anywhere."

I kiss her, tasting the champagne on her lips. I savor it. Commit everything about this night to memory.

Getting to kiss Alice like this is something I'll never get over. I'm so thankful she took that chance on me. Because being with her is everything I want.

"Good. Because you're stuck with me for life."

Bonus Epilogue

"You think she's doing okay?" Declan asks, staring down at the ice. "Are the other kids ahead of her?"

"She's doing great," I reassure him. "You have a higher standard than everyone else."

"Can you blame me?"

I rest my hand on his fidgety knee. "You're a retired hockey player. Just let her skate on her own level."

"I wouldn't be this nervous if you'd let me coach the team."

I try to stifle my laugh, but it comes bursting out anyway. "Declan, you know how the other parents would be. They'd accuse you of playing favorites."

"Not my fault if my daughter is the best." His eyes track Emma, now sitting on the ice, picking at the laces on her skates. "Why isn't she getting up?"

I drop my chin on Declan's shoulder and stare up at him. "Remember when we took her last week to break in her skates? You know she loses interest quickly."

"Froggie, don't jinx it. She's going to be the next best player in the women's league."

I watch as the coach helps Emma up and she skates—using the cone to support herself—to the bench. Her helmeted head bobs over the gate as she takes her seat.

Our four-year-old loves her dad more than anything. A daddy's girl through and through. When he retired after she was born, he started taking her to the rink with him to meet up with the guys. Emma decided then that she wanted to be a hockey player.

Unfortunately, she has my coordination. No matter how many times Declan tried to teach me to skate, I couldn't stay upright long enough. Maybe Emma will learn, but I know whatever she decides to do, Declan will love and support her.

Because he's the best dad.

"Practice is over," I say. "Come on."

Parents are lingering around the rink as they help their kids take off their skates.

"Did I do okay?" Emma asks, her face lighting up as she wobbles over to us.

"You did great. The best skater out there."

"Really?"

Declan nods, lifting her into his arms.. "Yes. You take after me."

"Yay!" She squeezes him. "Can we get milkshakes?"

"It's almost dinner time," I say.

"Absolutely." Declan ignores me as he starts walking to the car.

I can only shake my head at the two of them.

Emma has had Declan wrapped around her little finger since she came into the world.

"Then can we go pick flowers?"

Walking into the bright summer day, I slide my sunglasses over my eyes and nod at her. "Of course, sweetheart."

"Uncle Leon said our rannies might be ready."

I grin at her. Our ranunculus that we planted. She still can't say it. If there's something Emma loves more than skating, it's her garden.

She's the perfect mix of both of us.

"And maybe we can take them to Granny and Grandpa's?"

"They'd love that. Maybe we can take pizza over for dinner?" Declan says, turning back to me after buckling her into her car seat.

"I'll text your mom to see if they're home."

"Great." Declan drops a kiss on my lips as he opens the door for me. "I'm sure Emma will want to tell them all about practice."

"I know she will."

After we told Declan's parents that we were expecting, they decided to move to Denver to help out. Considering I haven't spoken to my parents in years, I love having family close by.

My phone buzzes.

"Your parents will meet us at our place."

"Want to grab them some shakes while we're out?"

"Sure."

As Declan steers us toward our favorite place, Emma recaps every minute of practice for us. I love it. Love that this is how we spend our days now.

A family of three.

I never thought that this would be my life. Married to my best friend, owning Enchanted Petals, and having the best daughter in the world.

By the time we get our shakes and get home, Kathleen and Aiden are waiting for us. Emma is giddy with excitement as she unbuckles herself and darts out of the car.

"Granny! Grandpa!" She bursts inside, finding them in the kitchen.

"There's my favorite girl."

Aiden picks her up, swinging her around.

"We got you milkshakes."

"You did?" Kathleen tickles her side. "You're my favorite granddaughter."

"I'm your only granddaughter." Emma giggles.

"And whose fault is that?" Kathleen cocks an eye in our direction as we walk inside, setting the drink carrier down.

"Don't look at me," Declan says.

He grabs his Styrofoam cup out of the cardboard carrier and stabs his straw through the lid.

"Way to throw me under the bus." I scoff.

"You know I love you, Froggie."

Declan throws an arm around my shoulders and pulls me close, pressing a kiss to the top of my head.

"See if I give you another baby."

"Let's not say that," Aiden says. "Emma needs a sibling."

Emma slurps down the last of her milkshake. "I want a puppy."

All of us laugh.

"You don't want a brother or sister?" Declan asks.

"I like playing with Puck," she answers. "He's fun."

"Maybe we should invite Cash and Piper over more often," I tell Declan.

"You know Cash will bring Puck. He loves that dog more than anything." Declan shakes his head.

"Maybe a dog and a baby?" Kathleen suggests.

"I want a dog," Emma says again.

"How about Granny and Grandpa get you one?" Declan says. "They can keep it at their house."

"Hey, now," Kathleen scolds Declan.

"Not a terrible idea," Aiden says.

"Really?" Declan and I say at the same time.

"I thought that would take more convincing," Declan says.

"Yes!" Emma throws her hands up in victory.

"Maybe you can help us pick one out," Aiden says. He pulls out his phone and, despite Kathleen shaking her head, they start looking at dogs.

"Well, that's one thing we don't have to worry about," Declan whispers.

I spin in his arms, linking my hands behind his back.

"Then how about we start working on giving Emma a sibling?"

"You think we're ready?" he asks. "You're busier than ever at the shop."

I shrug a shoulder. "Will there ever be a good time to have another kid?"

Turning, the two of us watch as Emma drags her grandparents outside to go pick flowers from her garden.

"Probably not."

"Then what are we waiting for?"

Declan waggles his brows at me. "You want to start now, Froggie?"

I swat at his chest. "Considering your parents are here, no."

"We could kick them all out. Put Emma to bed."

"At four in the afternoon?" I laugh. "Do you plan on getting up with her when she wakes up at three in the morning?"

He shakes his head. "Fair. I guess we'll just have to wait until bedtime."

I press a kiss to his lips. One that hints at what's to come.

"I can't wait."

Want more in the Black Diamonds? If you haven't started the series, check out Best Kept Secret now! Or start the Nashville Knights now!

Acknowledgments

BOOK THIRTY-TWO IS OUT IN THE WORLD!

I can't believe we're back with the Black Diamonds. I love this group of guys and loved getting to revisit them. I never thought I'd write this book, but when I sat down to plan my Patreon story for 2025, Declan snuck his way in and said "Hi! I'm here!" This story absolutely flew out of me and I loved writing it. This is such a beautiful ending to this series and I can't wait to see where we go from here.

A big thank you to Thuy (@tweezyreads) for helping me with the flowers…I loved all the beautiful suggestions you gave me to help bring Enchanted Petals to life.

Thank you to all the incredible readers, author friends, and everyone that picks up my books. I pinch myself everyday that this is what I get to do.

<3 Emily

Also by Emily Silver

Colorado Black Diamonds Hockey

Best Kept Secret

Best Laid Plans

Best of the Best

Best of Both Worlds

Best of You

Nashville Knights

Game Misconduct

The Playmaker

Breakaway

Bar Down

Toronto Rosebuds

Love Pucked

Toronto Rosebuds #2

Toronto Rosebuds #3

About the Author

Image by Tricia B @TheSmutFairy

USA Today Bestselling author Emily Silver was destined to be a writer after winning a Young Author award in second grade. She loves writing inclusive stories, with strong heroines and the swoony men who fall for them.

A lover of all things romance, Emily started writing books set in her favorite places around the world. As an avid traveler, she's been to all seven continents and sailed around the globe.

When she's not writing, Emily can be found sipping cocktails on her porch, reading all the romance she can get her hands on and planning her next big adventure!

Find her on social media to stay up to date on all her adventures and upcoming releases!